WHERE EELS LIE DOWN

A PARRAMATTA TALE

GARY CARTER

'It only takes a second to live in the past, present and future.'
To the memory of my pioneering ancestors, James, and Sarah McCooey.
They struggled on in the cycles of settlement.
This book is dedicated to the people of Parramatta, and the many cultures within.

INSPIRATIONS

Lake Parramatta

'Within this tapestry of human and environmental inter-action, that spans and bridges the past to the present, our lake stands out as a pearl in the multi-cultural oyster that is Parramatta. From a distance lake life has the twinkling symmetry of sunlight on water. It takes a closer inspection to see the wonders of nature and its contrasts.'

G J Carter

PROLOGUE

WHERE TRAVELLERS MEET

'Symmetries permeate nature.'

The Eel

The young eel larvae eat plankton to survive. They grow larger into glass eels with transparent bodies, evolution's protection from predators. They travel far, as they make their way to this great southern land and move into the tidal estuaries of creeks and rivers. When they reach one year of age they are known as Elvers. The travel continues into freshwater streams where they grow to adulthood and spend their lives. Mysteries surround their adventure. When nature calls a time for breeding, somehow most find a way back to their spawning grounds via creeks and puddles, they even cross the land to return, such is their determination. They then die in the raptures of procreation. Others may become totally landlocked and continue to grow to extreme size. Eels are good to eat, but large landlocked giants with needle sharp teeth must abound.

The Humans

The first arrivals:

There were other travellers to this giant southern land and lost in the long past were the details of the ancient journey they took. For them there were times when mountains erupted in orange horror. There were times when rains fell, and the creeks and rivers flooded. There were times when the dry land burst into flames following lightning strikes from angry clouds. They recorded all, in dreamtime tales of creation. For thousands of years, they lived with the land and what it provided. They witnessed the giant megafauna die out by fire, feasts, and climate change. They slept under the stars and hunted on days of constant blue skies. Women collected what was available from nature's store, while children played. The clans were plentiful despite the myth, it was not an empty land. Language was extensive and community boundaries were determined by the scaring ceremonies and secret rituals. It was a simple life of living with the land, not owning it. For in reality the land owned them. They all hunted, trapped, and fished; all food sources were used. The eel was a favourite of many clans.

Then the boats arrived:

There were times when hunger and greed overwhelmed the collective good and led, via debtors jail and prison barges, to penal colonies in the great southern land. Convicts trudged the bush, cut the sandstone and built roads and bridges for the new colony. The overseers, well trained Red-coat regiments of the mother country England, dished out punishment and pain as down payments for their burden and homesickness. Arthur Phillips first landing place at Sydney cove grew and within a year so did its food bowl at Parramatta, the colony endured. As the pain of settlement faded and the new colonial son's and daughter's took root in this hard and hungry dry land, hope rose to glory. There were times when peace and security came with the release of convict irons. That led to a new country with new laws and above all freedom. They went on to conquer the land, battle in wars and depressions. Their family trees were resplendent with shining medals of hope, sacrifice, and heroes. This great southern land blossomed with potential. When droughts persisted and crops failed new diets became a necessity. These same colonial boys would fish and hunt like the natives before them, for some the eel was a delicacy.

And still more boats came:

There were times when hope for a better life died with family and friends, when the horrors of war and hate went on without end. There were times when the status of refugee in a new country promised happiness and opportunity, where open arms beckoned to help build a lasting Eden in the spirit of peace. This would be the place that future wealth could be earned and spent on growth and play. As it was for the original inhabitants of Parramatta, clans like the 'Burramattagal', were content in the place where Eels rest.

Now on the horizon where the wind born detritus of life in a sunburnt country feed the schools of fish and eels in their survival patterns, more boats are coming. They are all full of these same fears but mixed with the hope of acceptance and achievement. We are all just fresh figures on life's canvas.

We are all just fearful and fearless humans seeking survival and acceptance. We are all windows of the same spirit, and we all end up at a place where travellers meet.

FORWARD

Rose and Thorn hotel Parramatta

Pub mates talk:

'Do you know Charlie when you get right down to it, right into the heart of the matter, it's all about being scared and coming out on top. Whenever the 'Black dog' of depression bites me, or a snake crosses my path, at first, I fear it, it's only then that I can control it.'

'You are dead right Jim, I use a country drive, or a bush walk as a weapon against the Dog. My other nemesis spiders I control with fly spray or a shoe. But jokes aside mate I also think that using fear as a weapon can help fill the void between anxiety and achievement. My dad used to say, the winds of fear and the tides of hope are what make us human.'

'It's that old fight or flight and strength in numbers adage, isn't it Charlie, sometimes heroes be afraid, and sometimes cowards have strength. Our similarities out-weigh our differences, we all have that moment when we win the game, and it's recognising it that brings success.'

'Spot on mate, it doesn't matter where we come from, we are all fearful and fearless, we're all heroes and villains. The symmetries are inevitable.'

CHAPTER 1

Harmony McCooey

'We paint our lives in the colours of the world around us. The brushes we use we inherit from our ancestors.'

A bright morning sun peeked over the eastern horizon and reflected on snow covered fields, as a multitude of chimneys belched out the black smog of warming fires. It was seasonally wrong for the 31st day of May in the year 1821 and despised by all, except possibly the sellers of the dreaded future climate destroyer. The ghosts of London's great history shivered along with the living populace. If they had have known it was to be the last end of May snow for 150 years, they may not have complained so much. It was also a day of regret, resolve and the start of an adventure for one Irishman and his future kin.

Harmony McCooey was shivering as he squatted on the deck of the prison hulk and looked out on the Thames. A now tattered rectangular woollen cloak and animal leather stitched boots barely kept the cold at bay but did mark him as one step up from the poorer convicts. His mind was on the outgoing tide, the rippling waves and fast currents now provided the only connection with his beloved Ireland. The thought crystallised like a snow-flake when he was startled back to reality by the jailers cry. His brief time in breathable air had come to an end, it was back to the boats belly and the dank smell of un-washed humanity perfumed with death.

Celtic ancestry had given Harmony fair skin, brown hair and a well-proportioned build that fitted well with his profession as a ploughman and farmer. But it was his stoic nature that would serve him best in the current situation. The one thing he needed to control was a fiery temper that ballooned out when he was painted into a corner. As he tried to sleep that night, the burden of his indiscretion weighed heavy on his mind. His thoughts were on the journey he had made to this state of living hell since the verdict was read:

'The jurors upon their oath present that Francis Har-mony McCooey late of the Saint Anne parish in County Down, did wilfully commit the said crime on the 27th day of February 1820 in the reign of our sovereign, King George IV. Then and there being found feloniously brutal had committed this wrongful act against the peace of our Sovereign Crown and Dignity.'

Fourteen years, the judge had decreed. It was in truth, he thought, an exile for life from his beloved Sarah and he knew it could have been worse.

On a cold crisp morning in February 1819 Harmony set off on his morning inspection walk carrying his scythe. He was looking forward to a small celebration for his birthday that evening. Sarah was going to prepare a spe-cial treat. He was approaching the Parish lands when he spotted a trespasser taking a short cut. Not knowing who it was at that stage and fearing a thief, he sought to warn the man of his intrusion. Suddenly he was set upon with a violent outrage and received a large laceration on his brow with the first blow from the trespassers cane. The Irishman's temper flared proportionately, and he gave the attacker a few defensive swipes with his scythe. The man went down in a cringing ball of pain and blood. Harmony calmed to tend to the man and realised at once it was the Anglican parson. He was a man of some standing in the community but known to have the odd tipple every now and then. He was in a sorry state both cut and drunk. Harmony had Sarah tend his wounds. On recovery the Parson looked beyond their kindness and submission of mistaken identity, he had Harmony arrested for assault.

The judge at Downpatrick frowned when the charges were read. Despite the trespass and the Parsons state of inebriation, he decreed that excessive force was used. It was revealed that the Parsons right ear was cut clean off in the struggle and fight over right of way and he would be scarred for life. No mention was made of Harmony's scars and the judge was in no mood to be lenient to what he termed, 'a bad-tempered Irish Catholic'. He transferred the case to the Old Bailey in London. Harmony was facing a death sentence. For three months he lingered in a cell at Newgate prison. A rare visit from Sarah and his father gave him a little hope. A family friend Lord Grafton had written a letter in his defence. It testified to the good character and excellent skills that Harmony had shown as the parish farm overseer. It saved him from the gallows, but the Old Bailey judge sentenced him to transportation. From Newgate he was transferred to a prison hulk on the Thames River. These prison hulks were convenient temporary holding pens for convicts awaiting transportation. They had no riggings, masts or rudders and were generally unseaworthy. The internal structures were reconfigured with jail cells. It was in one of these cramped and dismal cells that Harmony spent six months. To a man of basic education, the prospect of a trip off the edge of the world was a frightening thought. He curled back into the bunk with depression eating away at his thoughts.

Francis Harmony McCooey was born in Armagh County Ireland in 1788 the last of four boys. He grew up in a world of need. His mother or 'Ma', as he called her, named him Francis. His middle name Harmony came from his dad. A dad who believed that this beautiful blue-eyed son was special. With an extra thumb for luck, this boy would bring harmony into the McCooey family.

Looking from the front door of their thatched roof mud hut, at the age of eleven, all Harmony could think of was his 'Ma' and what he could eat. He shared one bed with his three brothers. Their main past-time was fighting each other, which occasionally earned them a backhand off their dad, as did failing to carry out chores. They had minimal Catholic schooling up to the age of fourteen, but could all read, write, and manage some arithmetic. Times were tough and a life of odd jobs, helping at home or an escape to greener pastures was all they had to look for-ward too. Harmony's older brother Patrick was also his best friend. Their main chore was following coal-carts and scavenging for falling pieces of coal. This would help keep the family warm on a cold winter's night.

In the summer of 1800 Harmony and Patrick were ex-cited about going with their Da to look for work around the harbour at Ardglass, one of the most scenic and quaintly beautiful towns in all of County Down. All the brothers had shared trips with their father over the years but now the two older boys had left home looking for work in Belfast. That meant life was a little easier and the younger two had more adventures. They arrived in town around lunch after a two-day trip and while their father asked around for work, the boys went for a walk to the hill-side cliff north of the harbour. It was an overcast day, and the Irish sea-mist was blowing in their faces. Harmony saw it first:

'Look Pat there's dinner!' he yelled.

A rabbit darted out from under the briar and both boys gave chase. It ducked and weaved through the scrub and rocks turning sharply in the opposite direction across the muddy paddock. The cows were not amused but Patrick was, as his laughter was electric. A hungry Harmony was determined to have rabbit stew for dinner and took several dives into the mud during the pursuit. It suddenly turned left and ran along the cliff edge. Harmony did not see the fresh cow dung adjacent an old oak tree and as he stepped into it, he skidded over the cliff edge. Patrick's eyes bulged in horror, and he ran towards the cliff. Harmony had luck on his side, he had somehow managed to grab onto a protruding tree branch as he went over the edge. When Patrick got there his white-faced brother was in a state of terror hanging over a sixty-foot drop. A local farmer who had been watching their antics came down to assist, between them they managed to drag Harmony back on to level ground. When his panting settled, he was still in a state of shock. His mind was now tattooed with a lifetime anchor, a fear of heights, it would never leave him. Their father was not amused,

'Your Ma would have blamed me!' he screamed.

'It surely would be the death of her if I were to bring home a dead son!'

He settled after a while and felt grateful that his son had survived. As it turned out the chance encounter with the farmer had led to an offer of work. The whole family moved to County Down where they prospered under a tenant arrangement with the farmer, a young Lord Grafton. Sadly, their mother died during childbirth that same year. It always played on Harmony's mind, that somehow it was his fault.

The ups and downs of life flowed on, and Harmony became a freehold farmer on his family's property 'Ravenswood' in Ballycoe County Down. The family had come a long way from their humble beginnings in County Armagh. They were considered well off by their Irish peers. The English 'Penal Laws' which were introduced to stop Irish Catholics from owning land were repealed in 1790. This allowed the family to pay off, through hard work and tenant farming, their small property. They lived adjacent to the Lands of the titled Lord Grafton, who in some ways had befriended them. The day to day running of the farm, tilling the soil, planting potatoes, and scything his and Lord Grafton's properties, kept Harmony busy and active. He was also overseer of the local Parish lands. In May of 1818 he married his lifetime love Sarah Kelly. One year later Harmony's life went off in a new direction.

Harmony had been in the hell-hole hulk for six months and witnessed the death of more than one of the suffering prisoners. The stench of death was still lingering when the depressing news reached his ears. The hulk jailers were feeding the fish with the bloated body of the most recent dead inmate, when their mutterings were overheard. The rumour bounced about the hulk like an apple in a barrel. The bulk of the prisoners were to be moved to a ship for transport to a god-forgotten place, called Sydney Cove.

A leather-bound writing journal, that Sarah had given him, was his most cherished companion. In it he scratched out his feelings and trials, it offered at least some release. The words 'On a ship bound for worlds end', were his latest entry, it summed up his feelings.

Harmony was a large man, when compared to his peers, but above average height was not a consideration to the builders of the prison hulk. The bunks were not built for comfort. He curled back into the tiny area and opened a letter from Sarah. There was a crack in the flooring above his head that let in a narrow stream of light. It was enough to allow him to read. He may never see his extended family again but there was hope that one day his wife could join him in the colony. Lord Grafton had mentioned this in correspondence. He was also preparing a letter to be sent to the Governor of the colony that may lead to an early release from the sentence. This could give Harmony a fresh start in a new land. It could be years before Sarah could join him there, but there was always hope. He would now spend his time worrying for her well-being. As to his own state of mind, the notion of distance was eating away at his soul. If he could name a good point of his situation, it was that no one, yet had made fun of the extra thumb on his right hand. He knew in his heart that God had chosen him for great things and the extra appendage was the almighty's signature to that end. His other distinguishing feature was the new scar on his right brow, complements of the vicar. It was a constant reminder for him to control his temper.

It was their last day on the Barge. Excitement of release from the hell hole and trepidation about a sea voyage away from loved ones blended in mixed emotions. Most of the barge convicts were prepared and taken for transport to a tiny brig called 'Isabella', under the command of Captain Melville. He was a Captain with a reputation from the Napoleonic wars as being tough but fair. The medical officer a Doctor Perkins, from the transport ship had come aboard the barge earlier to inspect the convict cargo. Anyone he thought too sick to transport were directed to a holding cell. The rest were shackled around the ankles and herded in groups of ten to the deck. Harmony's group was first in line. It was a steamy sweltering summer day and the fresh air from a sea breeze on deck offered a welcome contrast to the stench and oven like conditions below. Captain Melville and a guard from the ship were on the gang plank, as this first group approached. Despite their fear of the pending voyage there was an air of expectation. This led to some humour and chatter amongst the convicts.

The captain walked past the group with no expression, but the guard, with an ugly scowling face and a well-fed frame barked a command for silence. The first group went quiet as he walked on staring at each man, as if assessing their nature. When he came up to Harmony he had to look up, due to their height difference. This seemed to displease him. He then sneered and dribbled in Harmony's direction and told the whole group to sit on the deck. This ritual went on for the next two groups. Two sailors then came aboard with chains and tethered each group's leg irons. They were now as one and would be bound like this for the first two weeks of the voyage.

Discipline was a firsthand weapon to maintain order and this Captain was a Master of It. The guard returned to the first group and gave the order to stand. As he walked past Harmony the tethering chain tightened as the group stood. This caused the guard to trip in a blubbering mass onto the deck. Spontaneous laughter erupted amongst the convicts. There was no intent of malice, it was just laughter, a moment of joy in a mad world. Samuel Maitland the guard had a unique perspective, he had suffered humiliation in front of lesser men. He slowly rose to his feet and was expressionless as he stared directly at the Irishman. The face of this low life sniggering convict was fused in his memory. Harmony's smile faded as Maitland spat at his feet and snarled in a soft voice:

'Laugh now two thumbs, it will be your last bit of humour for eternity!'

He then continued to the front of the queue, grabbed the chain, and walked the first group across the gang plank like a pack of dogs. Harmony had made himself a powerful enemy through no fault of his own and was amazed at the guard's power of observation in relation to his thumb.

On the 15th of July in the year 1821, the Isabella set sail with a complement of three hundred cramped souls most of whom would never see home again. They were leaving a Charles Dickens London with a beautiful new bridge crossing the Thames River. It was a class society where the poor suffered and the rich reigned supreme. The Government official who oversaw convict behaviour while on board was a Mr Friend, he was not cruel, but he was tough and his name throughout the next six months was to become a cynical joke. From that day on Harmony's mates consisted of mind images and voices within the dark damp hull of the ship and of course the rats that did not bite.

The convicts all agreed that the ugliest and most horrid creature aboard the vessel was the prison guard from the barge encounter. Maitland had accepted his convict inspired nickname of Pug with the acrimony of one who knows his place in the scheme of things. He wore it like a medal, but secretly made a mental note of the convicts he detested most. Harmony made the top of this list. Most of the vessel's population thought that 'Pug' was just short for pug-ugly because only God in his wisdom could have made Maitland's looks synchronize with his soul with such perfection. A permanent scowl on his pock marked face, together with a birthmark in the shape of a crescent moon on his cheek, caused other convicts to cringe on his approach.

Samuel Maitland was born in Islington Village north of London in 1776. He would have been considered just an average child, but for one annoying habit. An allergy to mildew caused him to constantly sniffle and suck mucus to the back of his throat. He then dutifully disgorged the contents onto innocent bystanders. A habit like this tends to lead to many disagreements with friend and foe. So naturally Maitland went through life with scars, attitude and very few mates. Whenever possible Harmony avoided this creature, but like the rats on board, Pug had a knack of biting when you least expected it.

It was on the second week of the voyage and following the release of the tethering chains that Pug's attention focused squarely on Harmony. It was possible that jealousy of his height had brought on the instant disdain towards the Irishman. Or it may have been the perception that Harmony was responsible for the embarrassing fall aboard the prison hulk. Whatever the reason Pug took delight in degrading him to the other convicts as often as possible. The prime target of these attacks was his extra thumb and Pug's persecution was unrelenting. Behind the Captain's back he flogged Harmony for as much as sneezing. At other times food deprivation was his weapon. Harmony's pain became a ritual and his situation appeared hopeless.

'McCooey,' screamed Pug. 'Drag you and your extra digit out here into the light,' there followed a subdued snigger amongst some of the other convicts. The hatred between the two men grew daily and as the vortex of bitterness escalated Harmony pondered a solution:

'By voyage end,' he thought, 'This Pug would find his own true hell.'

He would use his own fear to trap this persecutor. The challenge that he now faced was to conquer his own demon, a life-long fear of heights. That was the only weapon he had apart from humour. He let the Pug pick up on this fear on a couple of occasions over a few weeks before arriving at Rio de Janeiro. A conveniently placed conversation with his bunk mates while the Pug was in ear shot did the trick and as expected led to further ridicule. The entrapment plan was in motion, all that was required now was some nasty weather. Harmony saw his chance on the evening they set sail from Rio.

Convicts make expendable sailors. Volunteers seeking extra rations were often sent aloft to secure rigging in dangerous weather. The rain squalls and high seas had come on quite unexpectedly only hours after leaving port. The Pug was told by Mr Friend via the first mate to send some volunteers aloft to secure rigging on the aft deck. McCooey was of course Pugs first choice as a volunteer:

'I can't do it Sir! I have the dreaded fear of high places, what if I should fall from up there.'

'Then fall you will, you two thumbed fool,' laughed the Pug. 'Get yourself up there or get the lash for supper, your choice. Now! swallow your fear and get moving.'

Harmony now saw his chance; the first mate was not watching. He swung his foot firmly into Pugs groin: 'Why don't you swallow those, pig!'

He grinned and in one motion began to climb. The Pug reeled on the deck in agony for a moment as his temper ballooned. He had taken the bait and began to follow Harmony aloft. The storms din covered the Pugs cursing and the rest of the crew were unaware of the pending battle above. Both was tiring quickly; the adrenaline rush of anger had started to subside. Pug now found himself well above the deck and just out of reach of McCooey's legs. Although he had no fear of heights his heart raced from exertion. His weight and poor health added to the thought that his pursuit may have been a folly. He had to act now, so with a white knuckled left-hand grip on the rigging he swung high and fast with his right hand and managed to grab Harmony's ankle:

'I've got you now, you Irish devil!' Pug yelled, with spittle dribbling from his mouth.

Harmony lashed out with his left foot, bashing at Pugs head with several quick kicks. He then started kicking the vice like grip Pug had on the rigging. Suddenly the grip released. Harmony now seized on the opportunity and swung his nemesis clear of the rigging dangling him over the exposed aft deck. The Pug now had no choice, he grappled at McCooey's legs with both arms. Again, Harmony lashed out at his enemies head. With luck now going his way he wrapped his arm over the yardarm and managed to hold on, despite the bloated weight hanging from him. Dangling in free space Pug tried in vain to climb up McCooey's legs. But the constant head bashing was taking its toll. Rain, blood, and salt leached into his eyes; the stinging intensity weakened his resolve even further. Harmony, sensing victory, used his free hand to pry open Pug's grip on his legs. With one last fear filled effort Pug Maitland bit down hard on Harmony's hand, severing his extra thumb in one bite. Harmony's scream was heard by all on deck.

It was too late for Pug Maitland his last thought was of McCooey's extra thumb stuck in his throat. He fell to the deck across a cedar chest, the mortal thud breaking his back and splitting his head. After a minute of writhing in intense pain he choked to death. Mr Friend saw the impact and ran to assist. It was obvious by the twitching and crushed body that he was beyond help. Harmony climbed back down to the deck and feigned empathy.

'What happened here McCooey?' Friend scowled in disbelief. 'You'll hang for this!'

'Please be to God Sir?' Harmony cowered. 'Mr Maitland saw that I was in difficulty and climbed to assist me in securing the rigging, bless his heart. You see Sir, I was overcome with the dreaded fear of heights. The ropes were slippery, and as he climbed to help me, he lost his grip. I tried Sir, I reached out, and he held on with both hands, and his mouth, but alas he slipped through my grip and fell Sir!'

'Did you say mouth McCooey?'

'Yes Sir,' showing Mr Friend the gaping hole in his hand.

The first mate gave McCooey a suspicious look:

'Get yourself down below, and have Dr Perkins tend to that wound. Don't be thinking that you are some kind of hero McCooey, I know you Irish. The captain will review this in the morning, and I'll be keeping my eye on you!'

The next day the Pug's body was ceremoniously fed to the sharks, with some prayers from the captain. After the service Perkins approached Harmony with a gift. The small formaldehyde filled glass jar contained a thumb:

'McCooey?'

'Yes Sir!'

'I retrieved this thumb from Mr Maitland's throat, I believe you acted in good faith, so you may as well have it as a keepsake to your good deed. You are a lucky man; the captain believed your story because of that thumb. He knows what sort of man Mr Maitland was, and that he would have bitten hard to save his selfish life.'

'Yes Sir,' Harmony frowned with solace, 'that he did Sir, he bit hard, and the poor fellow also hit hard.'

'Just one more thing Mr McCooey, I have a word of advice for you, Mr Friend still has his doubts about your story. So, keep yourself out of sight and out of mind if you get my meaning. It's a long voyage to Sydney cove, and you don't wish to follow Maitland into the fish food soup, do you now?'

'No Sir, that I don't.'

Harmony's eyes shifted for moment with a shadow of guilt, but he also smiled inwardly. Freedom from persecution was only part of the reason for his actions, the other part was choice. The Pug's of the world never give up, they chip away for a weakness and pounce. Harmony knew his own temper and what the outcomes would have been in a rush of anger. The hangman's noose would have ended any chance of freedom or seeing Sarah again. The Pug's agonizing death would haunt the Irishman for the rest of his life. But for now, his journey continued.

Throughout time and the tapestry of life and death, the seeds of good and evil weave their way in search of balance. The McCooey and Maitland clans would cross swords again at a future date because we are all victims of fate, fear, and finality.

CHAPTER 2

Jake McCooey

'From the wind, the fire, and the blazing sun, springs
the purple foliage from within the blackened gums'

When night fell, the sunset stayed, and fear
filled the void where stars once smiled. It
came from the mountains of blue, a fire ball
of noise that ate the trees and scarred the land. The terror was all consuming. All was still now, new life glowed
in the damp reflections of morning sunlight and a new
sound was heard down on the river. White ghosts with
wooden arms, moved their vessel slowly towards the
place where the Eel's lie down.

Gilpani sat on the sandstone boulder watching a long-
finned eel move around the lily pads. His sister was on
the other side of the creek casually foraging for berries
but keeping one eye on her brother. Pinacan like the rest
of the Burramattagal clan was proud of the skill Gilpani
had shown when using a spear. At that moment, he stood
as still as a tree on a windless day, positioned his feet
and threw the spear with the confidence of an elder. The
spear pierced the larger upper part of the yellow-backs
body, as it twisted in the pain of a death dance and mud-

died up the previously crystal-clear waters of the creek, Pinacan clapped with joy. On that same day she had also witnessed her brother snare a turtle and stalk to capture a goanna. She saw how Gilpani stood still and listened to the bush. When the yellow crowns of the cockatoos flared, they spoke with squawks of fear for their nested young, he reacted swiftly, followed the sounds of fury, and captured a goanna that was half his own length. Tonight, their family will feast in honour of Gilpani. He will then go with the fathers and return a man, his right of passage cemented by his skill.

In time's shadow, Jake McCooey, the progeny of Irish convicts, free settlers, and currency lads, some of whom took on Aboriginal partners, sat where Pinacan once stood. He was watching a young Asian boy fishing with rod and line in the shadow of Gilpani. As a boy, Jake found out that hiking in the bush was challenged by distance more often than time. Today, it offered more of an escape in a world gone mad with haste. His life was a full river of memories and as he approached the delta of its conclusion, he often found himself at his favourite retreat, the old blue gum tree by the lake. He was dressed for the season, shorts, tee shirt and walking shoes. He had with him an enjoyable book and an hour to kill. The creek and time had sculptured craggy sandstone caverns and bays, many of them were now filled with water held back by a man-made dam. The abundant trees in the Lake Parramatta Reserve filtered the morning sun, and its warmth helped focus his memories. Jake was having happy thoughts about their recent lottery win. Now, they could purchase, their dream home.

His family used the funds to buy back the home his great grandfather had built. The Goldstein family of solicitors had put the home, called 'Redrum,' on the market for the first time in eighty years. So, as if fate led the way, Jake and Anne bought it, and gave it back the original name 'Ravenswood'. The National Trust at first rejected the name change saying it reflected the English Redcoats and the Rum rebellion of the Macquarie years. But with a little research and a name reversal Jake established the truth. To criminal lawyers 'Murder' was money.

Built in 1856 by Melville and Sons, to his ancestor Harmony McCooey's own design, the house had an air of expectation. Lichen covered slate roof tiles and gothic finials shelled this stately manner. It stood now as the icon of Sorrell Street and a testament to past love and character. Originally named 'Ravenswood', after Harmony and Sarah McCooey's Irish cottage in Ballycoe. They would have beamed with pride on the day their new home was ready for occupation. Sandstone blocks and wide verandas gave it coolness, while vibrant coloured fascia's and fixtures gave it warmth. The acre of land was planted with a mixture of old English and Australian native trees. The circular driveway from the road wound past a latticed gazebo on the right and a 'frogs hollow' lily pond on the left. The entrance beckoned with invitation. Inside the two-story house a spiral staircase led to the four bedrooms. The master was the larger, with a sitting room and entry was via a grand hall with an off-set attic to the rear. The ground floor encompassed a nineteenth century kitchen, together with back-to-back fireplaces, one for kitchen warmth and in the past cooking, the other facing the lounge and living room, where the echoes and spirits of former lives, could be sensed even now. The place was a masterpiece of nineteenth century design.

The old family wealth was lost in the peaks and troughs

of poor investments, and the battles of sibling distribution. In contrast, Jake grew up in Westmead, just west of Parramatta, in a house provided by the government. It soon became a home filled with children. His hardworking parents paid it off quickly. They lived in a cheerful home with the fun of birthday parties and yearly camping holidays. His childhood was overflowing with great memories. As he approached puberty, life became adventurous and as with most teenagers in the sixties future ambition was in short supply. Excitement was always found outside and unlike the 'Net Nerds' of today, only mummy's boys and the sick stayed inside. Choices were scarce in the sixties, football or cricket on weekends, and scouts or police boys clubs during the week. The friends he made in those formative years stayed with him for life. Memories included abseiling and rock-climbing weekends at Katoomba, orienteering, canoe trips, white water rafting and hikes galore. Bravado gave fear no footing within Jake's circle of mates, at least up until a caving trip to Wee Jasper in the late sixties.

A local group of caving enthusiasts had invited his scout troop for a weekend of wonder, exploring the limestone caves around Yass. There was a narrow stretch of close rock between two large caverns 150-metres below the surface. The instructor had prepped the boys for the challenge and highlighted the wondrous stalactite encrusted cathedral in the second cavern. Their excitement peaked when he called for a volunteer to go first, Jake got the nod and crawled forward on all fours, wide eyed with the pleasure of the pending discovery. Despite the safety warnings and a situation awareness talk on the limits to their explorations, an adventurous Jake went a little too far. He was negotiating a turn in this bridging section of cave when the instructor called out to go left. Jake went right and got caught in a jam. As he struggled to free himself there was a small rock fall to his rear. The pleasure then blended with panic. No one got to see the second cavern that afternoon, it took two hours to free him. Claustrophobia sprouted roots in Jake's mind and caving was crossed off his list of fun things to do.

The caving experience did not stop Jake and his mates planning and executing weekend escapes. Their adventures would send some of today's parents to stress clinics. They would often take trains to various locations and go on push-bike hikes to places like Newnes, north of Lithgow. They would camp out on the grassed-over railway station, and then hike to the tar-pits left idle from the old shale mining days. On one occasion, the Publican from the iconic old Newnes Pub gave them their first taste of beer and as they looked around at the 'Playboy' nudes, that the owner used for wallpaper, they thought of themselves as men. All required a cold swim in the local creek to get over the effects of just one beer, and the refreshing ale took a hold for life.

Another adventure on a cold wet August night, in the late sixties, had them sleeping by a fire on Mittagong Railway station. The fire was lit by a kindly old station master, in the days when they had such people. The sun had not yet risen when the boys set out for Oberon 178-kilometres to the northwest. On street bikes with no gears and a knapsack strapped to the rack, achievement negated complaints. From Wombeyan Caves, then on to Oberon and a steam train trip from Tarana, clearing sheep off the line for a train travelling at a walking pace. The whole trip was a challenge that had its fair share of flat tyres, sore legs, and fun. The third night camping out proved to be the Mount Everest of the adventure. On a soft green patch of lawn 40-kilometres from Oberon, reality struck with a storm and a flash flood. The site turned into a fast-flowing creek, the tents into sails and the sleeping bags into rafts. The boys dragged everything they could onto higher ground. They stood there soaking wet and cold, scratching away with damp matches trying to get a fire going. They survived on laughter and bravado and to this day still relate to their boys own adventures.

Life's skills learnt at an early age, especially the old scout adage 'Be Prepared' came in handy when Jake's dad died of Leukaemia, at the early age of thirty-nine. Jake was only fifteen when at the wake an uncle made the mistake of telling him he was now the man of the house. For a while it was like he stepped out of himself and everything including life was speeding up. High school was a blur. He went to Arthur Phillip High School and most of his mates went to other schools in the area, but they still had their weekends.

Around this time, he met Anne, his first girlfriend from school. It took thirty-five years, two broken marriages and a New Year's Eve party for the new millennia to find each other again. Together they beckoned in a new era, hopeful for a world of peace. How wrong they were, the 9-11 New York terrorist attack was just around the corner, but they still had each other, dysfunctional warts, and all.

Two years later they married, both were fifty and life-wise from blended histories. Six months after the wedding they won a motza in Lotto, the big ball dropped on the happy couple. Like with the old saying 'Shit Happens' it seemed that luck happens also.

Jake secured an Electrical Apprenticeship after he left school and worked in the Electricity supply industry for most of his life. Like most baby boomers a secure job offered a steady income through the ups and downs in the economy. It also provided the job satisfaction of being there long enough to be a major part of the industry's growth. Most of the blokes that he worked with had been there for more than thirty years. The X and Y Gen new starters barely stayed three years in a job these days and tagged the old blokes as dinosaurs. The sad thing about a short stay in a technical job is the lack of acquired experience and critical knowledge that comes in handy when things go belly up. One of the first things on Jake's retirement 'must-have-list' was a portable generator. Within the next ten years most of the old blokes will have gone. As replacements are thin on the ground and attrition is all but a forgotten word, the future could be a dark place. Still a change in thinking in the way things are done is a possibility, but it is generally a slow process. As an old Engineer mate of Jakes used to say, 'The worm turns, and most of the time ends up where it started.'

The old company had changed its name many times over the last fifty years from its Local Council beginnings. Today's new name basically summed up the present mood of its customers. 'Energy Matters' is a company for the challenging future, the new glossy magazine stated. Well, the corporate consultant who came up with that line could be onto something. The control room at Energy Matters was a career cul-de-sac for most emergency operation staff. This group of people had worked together on the road and in the office for so many years that they were almost a family. This was more about a family that had a sign over the front door reading, 'friends welcome, family by appointment'. There was always a great deal of chest thumping because assertive controllers rely on ego to get things done, but serious fights were nonexistent.

The characters on this work stage went about the business of power supply with a detached indifference to the mushroom farm of coffee stop bureaucratic appointments, beyond the security doors. This was where real time was thought to slow down to a hibernation state. Concentration and workflow were taken seriously, but this did not stop it floating along on a river of humour and roasts. All the players had a list of nick names from past experiences, and they were not always politically correct. Most grew like weeds on the lawns of new management ethics policies. Friendly roasts and slagging were distractions from other personal problems that most men would not easily talk about. Shift workers are a breed of their own and divorce rates are high, so there is always someone facing a new challenge in life. Just like Jake did on two occasions, but the picture looking in from the outside was always that of a professional group who got things done.

Jake had more nicknames than he could remember, but 'Splash' stuck like the river mud that covered him when he fell off a ladder on a pole near the bank of the Colo River back in the eighties. The ladder required moving to a steadier location. So, while Jake hung on to a crossarm, his off sider moved the ladder. It was not a wise move as the ladder fell and split in two. Jake's arm hold was fading fast, and repairs were too slow, a swan dive was imminent. It turned out to be a bellyflop, the water was cold and luckily deep.

The biggest shite stirrer was Sam Sullivan, 'Sully', 'Sullage' or 'Sulky' always got his attention. He was one of those blokes who could give it all day but hold a grudge for a week if the payback stung too much. Others included 'The Admiral,' he had all the answers and the officer's walk. Everyone had a tag; it could be a cartoon character or based on an incident with a humorous story attached. One such story related to a bloke they called 'Dildo.'

Emergency Power and Water workers rate well down in the pecking order of the community service groups like Police and Fire, but their presence is required on most occasions. Car impacts, bush fires, floods and storms are constants in our everyday world, and often some of these other emergency groups are first on the scene. Then there were the run-of-the-mill house calls, for things like blown fuses, crook light fittings and noisy meters etc. Bruce Kirk was a straight talking and serious sort of fellow, who hid his emotions well. He had spent an hour on a noisy meter complaint trying to locate a problem, but there was no discernible noise at the meter box. The lady of the house was insistent that there was a noise in her bedroom behind the bed. It was on the same wall that backed onto the outside meter box. Her husband was not home, and Bruce was reluctant to inspect the power point behind the bed. She was in a stressful state and felt it was a safety issue, so Bruce relented and crawled under the bed to look at the power point. There was nothing plugged into it, but there was a vibrating noise. A ten-inch battery operated vibrator was stuck between the bed head and the wall. He dislodged the offending item and crawled out from under the bed. As he handed it to her to switch off, the husband entered the room. The 'happy-to-be-home-from-work-smile' faded fast. The wife went as red as a beetroot, and Bruce as calm as ever said: 'happy to be of service Ma'am,' and left as quick as he could. The 'Dildo' nickname stuck for a long time after the story leaked.

Jake's early years contained great memories. These thoughts always flowed when he was in a quiet warm spot, like having a bath, sitting in the sun at the beach, or by a lake. He was totally relaxed as he sat there on the lake's edge. He had slipped his shoes off to soak his walk wearied feet in the cool water. He was staring at the reflecting ripples on the lake's surface thinking of all the events of the last month. Luck had certainly played a big part, but there seemed to be more to it, some sort of destiny thing. He was not one who believed in that mumbo-jumbo psychic stuff, but the connection to his family's history and the house purchase had him thinking. It occurred to him that water, whether it was a lake, a river or an ocean was a common connection with every life-form on the planet, past and present. This also included his ancestor Harmony, and the journey from Ireland.

A broken stick noise on the track caused Jake to look up. A strange looking bloke was walking at a quick pace towards the café. He looked to be around forty with black greasy hair and a nervous facial twitch or tick, like that of a cocaine addict. One feature that stood out, apart from the ugly scowl on his face, was a moon shape birthmark or mole on his cheek. He was dressed like he had just come from a Gypsy-Pirate pantomime or a part in a Johnny Depp movie. He was wearing a light grey patchwork baseball cap, on backwards, a pair of khaki army daks with a tucked in black tee shirt scrawled with white skulls. Bright red braces with mid-eastern motifs held the daks up. What complimented his garish attire was a wide studded black belt and black leather slip-on shoes with no socks. This exposed a leg strap of the type that would support a sheaf knife or perhaps gun holster, either way Jake knew that this bloke carried an unwritten sign that read, 'do not disturb.' Their eyes met and Jake, although in check, still offered a smile and a 'G'day'. There was no response, instead two dark eyes looked straight through him as he walked on at a quickened pace. This made Jake feel like he was disturbing the stranger's space.

It took a while for Jake to settle and get back to his book. Eventually the warm day won out and his relaxed mood once again kicked in. When he thought about it, the stranger could have walked unnoticed down the Parramatta mall on any day of any week. It was only in the bush that this twitching fish seemed to be out of his pond.

CHAPTER 3

The Rose and Thorn

A dry wind blew out its last breath of drought, as El Nino bid adieu. Amid sunsets of storm noise and lightning flashes La Nina flushed in. Talk of Desalination Plants faded almost as fast as the green grass made its long-awaited rebirth. Little white mushrooms poked their heads above the verdant green fields of Parramatta and the smell of cuttings lingered on. Magpies were beak diving mounds of damp dirt, feasting on Lazarus worms that were wriggling just under the surface, while 'Dylan' blared out on a distant radio:

'The times they were a changing'.

The twice weekly mows were back in fashion and Steve's lawn mowing cash flow was now in flood. There was a smile like the 'Luna Park' gate on his well weathered face, as he waited at the bar of 'The Rose and Thorn' for his mate Jake to arrive. It was Thursday night, raffle night, beer night, best night of the week and his mood matched. A dip in the lights from a distant thunder crack heralded Jake's arrival. This seemed to blend perfectly with his laconic, 'G'day mate!' as he pulled up a chair next to Steve.

Jake looked around the room, it was the usual bunch of locals. A scattering of Brokers, Real Estate agents, Landscape gardeners and Backhoe drivers. The afternoon crowd was growing fast. There was a famous well-known Cricketer trying to remain obscure and punting in the corner. There was a couple of regular soaks that seemed to live here. They all gave a cursory nod. On the far side of the room Jake could see that Charlie Stark, the whispering ghost was in his regular corner. He was a tall, long-haired, beer bellied mystery, with a pasty face. Even though they shared a mate in Jim Booth, seeing this depressed soul in the pub always gave Jake the creeps. Like the guy with the hunched back answering the door to a haunted house, Jake always felt the need to give him a wide berth.

Some of these blokes must have had great jobs, working less than four hours a day. They were always coming from lunch at a local restaurant or from quoting a new job. At times Jake thought he was the only one who worked an eight-hour day. The lotto wins only paid for the house and some renovations. Jake still had a few more years to go with the power company before he could even think of retirement, but it was a great feeling to sink a cold one after a hard slog and the social pill called beer was easy to swallow.

Thursday night at the Rose and Thorn was always packed. The colloquial terms of acknowledgement ran through the crowd as fast as the beer was poured. There were Johnos, Gazzas, Bazzas and Eccas. Other nick names were iconic like Bro, Cuz or Sport and there were also acronym names like ICE, meaning 'In Case of Emergency' you could always count on him. The lady drinkers did not seem to attract tags, but most were not backward in coming forward. Pub fools were called Keg-heads and the newcomers Blow-ins. It seemed your status as a Blow-in ended when someone added an A, O or Y to your surname. Of course, there were other less politically correct terms of endearment, but in general they all showed a warmth and camaraderie in conversation or quiet solitude. To most patrons having a drink and talk was a means to off-loading their daily burdens, troubles, and deeds in a way that Psychologists would term, 'being part of something bigger than self.'

Due in part to the good management skills of the publican Paul and his street wise staff, there were seldom any fights at this well sponsored watering hole. The Rose and Thorn was one of the oldest continuous drinking spots in Australia. The rum drinkers of 1823 differed only in smell, height and accent to the beer drinkers of 2000, their ghosts now rubbed shoulders across time but within the same space and this gave the place a sense of stability in a mad world. Some of the ancient Anglo Aussie's have been having a sip at this Pub for more than forty years as did their fathers before them.

They considered it the 'Rourke's Drift' of iconic Aussie pubs in the Parramatta area. The only thing missing was a name sign over their favourite chair. The meat and money draw were the big calling card on Thursdays and occasionally the money compounded to ten thousand dollars. Some of the patrons did not need it, most did, and some could not afford a food ticket without forgoing a beer. Nobody stood on ceremonies in this place. There were shit stirrers, quiet blokes, loud mouths, punters, and drunks. Outside you could wear a business suit or a T-shirt and thongs. Inside all were naked to their value.

Jake got on well with most of the blokes and ladies. At times he was too sensitive for his own good. He could be either a shoulder to punch or a shoulder to cry on. Tact was not his strong point, often he would get straight to the heart of it, like it or lump it. He saw himself as a six-foot punching bag with a hundred kilos of dreams; the pot belly did not count, for that is where he stored his empathy over discussions of sport and politics. This was his local watering hole and he loved to share it. Today when Jake looked back on his youth, the discussions almost always returned to footy or cricket. Even now in the autumn of his life, sport was still the glue of conversations in the absence of intrigue, mystery, or rumour. The story of the Lotto win and the purchase of the old joint up the road, had kept the gossip fires burning for months. Jake managed to quell the fire a bit with some well-placed shouts as down payments on his luck and to show he was still the same bloke despite coming into a little money.

'How's it going Jake?'

'Well, as good as can be expected Steve, if I don't go on about all the unnecessary bull that the historical society goes on with. I bet they would try to stop me from weeding the garden if they could. I just wish they would get the message; we have no intention of changing the character of the old joint. Both Anne and I love it just the way it is.

The name change thing really got up their noses, hopefully it will settle down now that the case has been won. Apart from that, Anne is having problems with her Mum now. Well, that's enough of my troubles, what about you Steve?'

'By the sounds of it surprisingly good, at least compared to you. I'm on an upper mate this weather is great for business.'

Steve Burns had been a mate of Jake's since they were five. At one stage in his life, he had made it to the dizzy heights of success, as a partner in a local firm of solicitors. After a soul-destroying marriage breakdown because of too many long lunches with too many ales, his life went down the toilet. It appeared he was well on the road to becoming just another 'Hungry Jack' and sleeping on its namesake doorstep begging for handouts. Recently Steve started to bounce back. He had weekend access to his kids and enjoyed being involved with their sporting adventures. He had also kick started a new business venture in the art of mowing lawns.

With pool balls kissing in the background and the room laced with laughter, Jake felt the mood,

'I thought that grin of yours said more than just hello.'

'Yeah, I'm up to me eyeballs in work.' Steve continued.

'I've been mowing twelve to fifteen bloody lawns a day. If this keeps up, I may have to hire some help. I think I'll give dopey old Marvin a call?'

He pondered half asking and half telling.

'I wouldn't bother mate, I heard Marvin is in a rut, apparently he had a run in with a keg head called Harvey Maitland, now he has locked himself in his unit, listing all the things that make him angry.'

'All the things that make Marvin angry could fill a novel Jake!'

'Well Steve, Anne has a friend that lives next door to him, and she thinks he's lost the plot and thrown away the head stone. Seems he never stops whingeing about all the rubbish that vacating tenants dump on the council strip next to the bus stop and how the buses never run-on time. It turns out that he read some article about a guy who wrapped a message of hope in a watertight container and chucked it in the ocean off the 'Gap'. Now dopey Marvin has got it in his head to record all his woes on a computer disk, wrap it up securely and peg it into the deep end of Lake Parramatta.'

'Bloody hell Jake, he sounds like a case for the Cumberland Mental Hospital.'

'Ah! It gets better Steve. He reckons in a thousand years from now, the old dam wall will give way and all the human excrement of shopping trolleys, car bodies and general unwanted crap will flood the valley.'

'What and somebody will find his bloody memoirs of misery!' Steve laughed.

'That's about it mate,' continued Jake. 'If you ask me, he is a bloody sad case.'

'Yeah!' mused Steve, tongue in cheek, 'does he really think people will still have a means of playing his stupid disk in a thousand years? Crikey I have had four or more different recording gadgets in fifty years, let alone a thousand! I think I will give him a call him anyhow Jake the recent storm activity may have fused a circuit upstairs. You never know a bit of mowing nature might change his outlook and get his mind off all that rubbish.'

'What about asking that goofy Irish mate of yours if he wants a job?'

'No Mick's still working for the Leagues Club, calls himself the assistant physiotherapist, truth is he just massages all the footy muscle after their pre-season work-outs.'

'Hell Steve, it's just summer and your talking footy already, give us a break, surfs up!'

'Yeah, I know what you mean, but our boys are professionals now and it is a twelve-month season, give or take a few resort holidays.'

'Well, it looks like Marvin's your man then.'

'Yeah, we'll see.'

'Speak of the devil, here comes Mick now.'

As Mick approached, the creaking pub floorboards brought about the usual round of 'pardon me' fart humour.

This almost always prompted the story of a fight between Midget O'Farrell and a giant named Peni Pitui. The big Islander went crashing through the floorboards, due more to gravity than the Midgets push. Poor old Peni crushed a cellar keg and broke a leg. This all occurred some years back in the days of the 'six o'clock swill,' before stained floorboards gave way to carpet and the renovations that led to the main bars present position. Some say in the dead of night you can still hear Peni's screams and the patron's laughter as the 'Midget' rose through the hole in the floor like 'The Phoenix' with a giant grin on his gob, splattered with blood and splinters in his forearms and bragging 'Who's next?' Sydney hotels all have stories of mischief, mayhem, blood, and vengeance, they also have a fair share of ghostly yarns, the Rose and Thorn was no exception. It is a fact; old pubs have memories of their own.

Mick Magee along with Steve were considered the pub's

biggest soaks. One of their other mates Bob Stickles, was a confirmed tea drinker, who constantly worked on their errant ways, trying his best to get them to ease back a bit. Most people thought that was a big task and did not hold out much hope. Mick was a ten quid import from Belfast. Back in the seventies, he along with his adopted family escaped the religious rivalry and the bombs that had killed his parents. The scars of that loss ran deep within him.

It was supposed to be a happy occasion that night at the Crown pub in Belfast. Everyone in the bar seemed friendly but as they left to the contrasting world beyond the swinging doors, a world where black cabs took the Shankhill Road, and two blocks away other black cabs took the Falls Road. A car bomb parked in front of the Europa Hotel stole their happiness and left their son with a bitterness born of constant hate. At the time, this hate was the currency of Northern Ireland and to some, at the time, a land well worth leaving for safer shores.

At the age of thirteen he arrived in Sydney with his Aunty Peggy and Uncle Joe, toughened by his experience but with a large slab of chips on his shoulder. Over the following years these chips were knocked off one by one within the emerging gang society of inner Sydney. It was the time of Skin heads and Sharpies. The constant fights and drama wore away at his need to escape the past violence in his life. At the age of sixteen he left school and seemed to give up the fight. He headed off down the unpaved road of hard labour, booze, and weekend rugby league. Along the way he picked up some skills and some muscle and this secured him a job running out messages and water to the players on the paddock and rubbing them down after the big game or training. By the time

Parramatta won its first Grand final in 1981 Mick had taken up residence in a pub room at the Royal Oak and bid farewell to Joe and Peggy who were heading back to Ireland, truly homesick although loving Australia.

'G'day boys, how's it going?'

'Just great Mick!' responded Steve.

'How are the EEL's faring?'

'They're shaping up all right for next season. We just signed up a new front rower from Fiji. He is a big boy with a big ticker and smart. We expect he will be 'State of Origin' material.'

'From the recent buys Mick, it sounds like Parramatta will be muscling their way to the grand final next year.'

'You could be right Steve, but even with the salary cap and our available cash running out fast, the back line is shaping up as a tight and talented unit as well. Expect some headlines next year mate. Anyhow enough football, I'll get us a round, same as usual?'

'Yes, thanks mate, a man's not a camel!' laughed Steve.

As Mick made his way to the bar there was a sudden disturbance at the table of a local couple. Matt and Samantha were watching in horror as their beer glasses moved with a will of their own towards the edge of the table. A table, that just happened to be the spot where Midge O'Farrell met his fate. An old local called Ecca grabbed the glasses a moment before they walked off the table's edge.

'Ya better hold on to these!' he mused, 'it looks like old Midge is on the move again.'

His casual attitude was in striking contrast to the couples wide eyed astonishment. It seemed that not all the spirits were served from bottles in this pub.

About a month after big Peni Pitui fell through the floor and broke his leg, 'The Midge', as he was referred to, by friend and foe, met with a gruesome end. The Midge was a bad gambler and owed a lot of people a lot of money. The bar was table free in those days and on this night, it was tightly packed with patrons. No one saw the knife that sliced through Midges rib cage and into his heart, nor did they see the murderer. But they all saw the crumpled body in a pool of blood lying near the cellar trapdoor. Some suspected Peni, but he was laid up with a broken leg at his house and the Police investigation led to a dead end. The stories of ghostly encounters began around this time and most of the patrons knew it was just 'The Midge' trying to get his hands on a free beer to drown his revengeful spirit.

Mick walked back to the table, beers in hand, with a new story to tell. A bit of mystery was always a bonus on pub night. A few beers later and after some long-winded speeches about team selection the talk started to fade. No one won the Thursday raffle, it jack-potted to next week, so Jake called it a day. As always, the conversation lingered for the 'one for the road', Mick wore the last shout and Steve's chatty happy mood continued.

'Are you and Anne still going to Terrigal this weekend Jake?'

'Yeah, mate and looking forward to it. Anne needs the break to take her mind off her mum's problems and I will help with a bit of wine, dine, dance and hopefully surf. There's a good swell pending!'

'Now what's all this strife about Anne's mum?' Steve asked as an afterthought.

'Not now mate,' as he sculled the last beer, 'I best be off, catch up next week. If you see Marvin, tell him to give me a call!'

As expected, Steve and Mick lingered for one more drink and Jake left with the ghost story now spreading through the bar, like beer from a cracked keg.

As Jake walked home from the pub in the fading heat of day, there was a hint of jasmine in the air, enhanced by the damp aftereffects of the passing storm. He felt a slight twinge in his right knee. It served as a reminder to his short-lived place in the scheme of things. Nothing lasts forever so all you can do is enjoy the moment and that is just what he intended to do tomorrow, after a good night's sleep. He was near the intersection of Sorrell and Grose streets when he had a strange feeling that he was being watched.

At first, he thought it may have been one to many schooners, but as he turned to look back towards the pub, ten metres away under a streetlight walked the pasty-faced Charlie Stark. The hairs on the back of Jake's neck stood up and tingled. He picked up his pace a little and saw Starkey take a right down Grose Street. That gave him a little relief, but as he thought about it, he was puzzled as to why the creep bothered him so much. Perhaps it was all in his head, what he really needed was just a good night's rest.

CHAPTER 4

Winter

A dark tunnel of claustrophobic and obscure thoughts filled his mind. Hidden problems, unresolved and unforeseen within Jake's dream or nightmare led somewhere. Deep inside a cavern of fear, a noise, a grinding machine, and the sound of turning continued. A scare, a movement and a rat run crazy across his foot. A startling awakening in a night sweat, as Jake rolls on his side and smells a sweet perfume. He whispers his dream into Anne's ear before it escapes back to the subconscious. Jake smiles at the recall, as the dream collates into a genuine experience.

When Jake was thirty, he had a young family and a troubled wife. He was unaware at the time that his wife Karen was having an affair. While on a night shift in the dead of winter his anxious mood somehow sensed a pending problem.

As an electrical field officer Jake and his assistant Dave provided first response to failures in western Sydney's vast electrical network. An intrusion alarm from the Carlingford transmission station was received and they were asked to attend. As they made their way through the outside gate and up the two flights of stairs to the control room, a constant soft banging noise was heard. The lights were switched on and two startled swallows flew straight at Dave's head and out through the door and an open window in the hall. The shock of this caused Jake and Dave to jump clear. They sat there, on the cold concrete floor, with bemused looks on their faces that slowly made way to smiles.

'I can see the headlines now,' said Jake, 'Two grown men scared by crazed swallows in local power station.'

'Or worse,' said Dave, 'young man dies of heart failure, scared to death by a bird!'

As Jake sat there, he looked around the room and noticed the old Bakelite phone on the table.

'You know Dave there must be a lot of history in a place like this, you can almost feel and hear the ghosts of past conversations. It has a real nostalgic feel about it, think about the number of hands that have picked up that phone or the footsteps on those worn stairs down to the basement.'

'Don't start Jake, this place gives me the creeps, always has, it feels like its haunted.'

Jake's mind was now racing, 3.00a.m in the morning, on a cold dark night in a haunted powerhouse. What a suitable place to challenge his fear of enclosed spaces and offer some distraction from his pent-up anxiety. It would also kill some time on a slow night.

Three floors below, large caverns cut into the earth, once housed giant synchronous condensers. Being rotating machinery, they were buried deep and vented to avoid noise that may upset the locals. These days all that was left of this old technology were a few nuts and bolts, some steel supports and three dark and brooding tunnels. Lighting had been removed twenty years prior.

Dave was grateful to return to the truck and monitor for further calls, while Jake descended the basement stairs. A slight breeze was blowing causing a soft whistle throughout the whole complex. There was also the background hum of transformers and the occasional click of relays. He could smell the dank dampness of unused space mixed with the scent of industry and there was another odour, urine. He cursed the dirty scum who had taken a lazy leak in lieu of using the provided facilities. As he moved on to the lowest level of the building, the light faded behind him. The view in front was that of a black curtain, it drew him in. Deep inside the middle cavern it was so dark and still that his eyes failed to adjust to the lack of light. The hairs on the back of his neck were now tingling.

Forever unknown to Jake was the presence of a harmful creature in the shadows. Evil eyes were trying to focus on Jake's every move. As he stepped forward into the dark, the sweaty hand of this particularly nasty being reached for his knife. A young vagrant with a hard heart awaited discovery, indifferent to the outcomes of life and death.

It was dead calm and coal black. All Jake could hear was his own shallow breathing as his cave fears returned. At first the temperature felt constant but in that moment of complete isolation it suddenly became cold. His threshold of fear was about to be tested. As he turned to retreat there was a slight breeze and the sound of a movement to his right.

'Is that you Dave, ya smart ass?' Jake enquired.

In that moment of no response, he walked back towards the light and the noise, thinking to startle his mate in return. With the next step and just as the edges of his vision were returning, a rat the size of a possum ran across his foot. Jake bolted, up the worn stairs in a flash and out to the truck. His mate was dozing at the wheel. He did not say a word he just sat with a smile on his face.

Dave looked up and smirked, 'scared yourself, didn't you?'

'No mate just exploring'.

Jake had controlled his fear and an inner part of him felt a strange relief that one of his demons had been put to rest. Even his anxiety about Karen had dropped off a little. Was he being paranoid about his wife's behaviour? A decision was made he would confront her and take the outcomes on the chin, good or bad.

The outcomes for Jake may have been different if he had taken another step in the cavern. Either way, the caverns temporary resident was not concerned. He put his knife back in its pouch and smiled at the intruders luck.

Jake was not always so lucky. When he finally confronted Karen with his suspicions it turned out to be bad. Karen left him and the kids. The shock was overwhelming. Her desire fell from him as do dead leaves from trees in winter, lying around until swept up on a windy day, neither here nor there just blown away. Ultimately the memories and sad songs of their breakup made way to warmer days and in this summer bush fire of emotion his past passion fled to new attractions. As a testament to the healing power of new love, settlements and vindictiveness ebbed with time and the extended family was made whole again, although scattered, it endured.

Jake learnt some valuable life lessons that were summed up by a councillor, some months later. He was clinically told a hard truth by a sweet lady, she said,

'All marriages can collapse under the pressures of family pain and finances Jake. But often the weight of poor communication can cause a selfish exit when grass looks greener elsewhere. Lives with partners old and new are all stories and add to the novel of our time. We are all victims of chance, choice, and selfishness. It's these experiences and memories that help make us who we are, warts and all.'

Time moved on, as did the pain for all involved. There were new stories and happiness ahead. In his present day, Jake realised his haunting dream came back to help him through his current family challenges and offer answers. The subconscious mind was always working away at life's problems. His dream was part of a lifelong learning and healing process.

The challenges facing the vagrant in the Carlingford substation on that winters night, were less complicated than Jakes, his were based on simple survival. Within the dark cavern he crawled back into his worn bedding seeking refuge from the cold, oblivious to the scurrying rats and their occasional bites. Before dawn he had his swag packed and was on the move once again. He exited the cavern through an old air vent, into the scrub at the rear of the substation. Patrick Maitland had discovered this entry in happier childhood days before bitterness took his life into the void of self-pity.

Somewhere, way back in the river of time, the dice throw of chance manifested evil into the mix of human nature. This genetic change for the worse, spread like a cancer growth through certain branches of humanity. The large family tree trunk of society had its roots deeply embedded in the good or evil traits of the past lives from which we are all descended. A sample of the evil lineage now took the form of this pathetic creature Maitland. He was a resentful and bigoted man living his life on the edge of society. The life skills he possessed always centred on connivance and how to secure other peoples hard-earned gains with a minimum of work. But his efforts however always seemed to lead down poverty's path, due to the volatile mix of jealousy and alcohol.

Survivor was the only positive word that could be used to describe Pat Maitland, all other attributes were negative.

CHAPTER 5

Harvey Maitland

'A cloud of evil floated by and stayed
with him till the day he died.'

Harvey's Aunty Trish gave his sister Sally a second-hand handbag for her eighth birthday and she loved it. There was nothing exceptional about it, if anything it was rather plain, a bit like Sally. At least that is what Harvey would have thought. When the bag was over Sally's shoulder it would reach the floor and if she knelt, she could almost hide behind it. It was made of shiny black vinyl and overlaid with two white bands of canvas material. Harvey's recall of it was remarkable he could even remember thinking at the time that it probably spent the best part of its life in someone's wardrobe. He speculated that Aunty Trish was always going to garage sales, so she most likely bought it for herself, had second thoughts and gave it to Sally. No one really said anything at the funeral as to why Sally would take her own life that way, but Harvey had his thoughts. He never really liked his sister that much anyhow.

Three days after Harvey's tenth birthday his window

cleaning father Doug took a sky dive from the top floor of the old Anthony Hordens building in Sydney. Doug had had a passion for heights from an early age he also had a fear of its attraction. Window cleaning and sneezing were poor companions, he had a family history of congested sinuses caused by grass and mould allergies. Windy days were the worst. His accident occurred on such a day when a passion for height and rye grass pollen in the wind all came together with a change of cleaning position and the mother of all sneezes.

Unlike today's Work Cover and litigation society, the only help the Maitland family got was some sympathy from friends. That included Uncle Ray helping himself to most of the tools in the garage. Doug's only other brother Pat did not even show up at the funeral. Other handouts to come out of the death were some window cleaning products and a free funeral, compliments of the sympathetic window cleaning company. There was no point in being bitter, at least the government let them stay in their Housing Commission home at Mays Hill.

A few months later Harvey's mum Jill had a nervous breakdown and was taken to a country retreat, at least that is what the welfare people told the kids. It was the St John of God Hospital at Kurrajong. Aunty Trish and Uncle Ray came to the rescue and gave Harvey, Sally and Jess a roof for the time it took to repair their mum. They all loved their eccentric Aunty. She made chocolate crackles and toffee apples on Saturday mornings and was always on hand to help at school fetes and functions.

Trish and Ray only ever had one child of their own. They named him Goliath due to his twelve-pound birth weight. He was the same age as Harvey but unfortunately was born with a rare brain disorder that was untreatable in the sixties. At the age of sixteen he became uncontrollable at home and despite the guilt and anguish Trish gave him up and had him committed to the Cumberland Mental facility at Parramatta.

For some reason Sally and Jess never warmed to Uncle Ray's warm hands and insincere smiles. In later life when their Mum would invite Trish and Ray over for a BBQ, they always made excuses not to attend. Harvey was never bothered by his 'touchy-feely' Uncle Ray as he always had his measure in smarts, muscle, and toughness. He preferred his Uncle Pat as a mentor, his dad's brother. Although he was a local sleazebag and bum, Harvey felt they had more in common and Pat knew how to make easy money. Harvey was rarely at home in those high school days, often wagging school and carrying out petty crimes.

During the time spent at Aunty Trish's, Harvey took Goliath under his wing. In a strange 'master-slave' way they became quite close. Harvey called him Golly and they were always off somewhere up to skull doggery. Golly was a gentle giant on some days and a mad ass nut case on other days. This blended with Harvey's withdrawn state of mind and the antics amused him.

They got into rock fights with local kids, they hid behind trees and threw old lemons, and rolled up papers at passing traffic and they blew up letter boxes with double bungers. They would often go on long walks around the local area exploring mischief. Down at the river or at the car park at Lake Parramatta they would get into fights with new Australian kids. The scars and bruises from these encounters were their war medals of honour. Aggression and defence became the normal routine. On some occasions, Harvey even found himself defending Golly against other kid's cruel comments. This big brother role gave Harvey a sense of being needed in a world of want.

While other kids became super-heroes like 'Superman' and 'Batman', they called themselves super villains, 'Harvey Hate' and 'The Golly Green Giant'. On some adventures they were cowboys, at other times they were pirates. They would carve skull and cross-bone effigies on the sandstone walls in over-hanging caves down at the lake. On occasions Harvey's manipulation of Aunty Trish would see him and Golly having a sleep out in the caves on the pretence of staying at another mate's house. At twelve years of age their hormones began to kick in and as their strength grew so did their bravado.

On a bright spring day in the September school holidays. Harvey had Goliath digging for a pretend treasure of gold nuggets adjacent to their pirate cave. That euphoric childhood feeling of fun times ahead was running on a full tank. Golly was doing his 'mad-dog' routine, dirt and shrubbery was flying every which way. Harvey was rolling around belly laughing at the antics, when suddenly there was silence. Golly disappeared.

Harvey stood back in shock, as it looked like the ground just swallowed his mate. The Golly Green Giant had landed chin first on a large slab of cold damp rock. Harvey peered in through the hole. A cloud of dirt and debris partly obscured his view but two metres below he could just make out the spread-eagled shape of his unmoving mate.

'Are you alive?' Harvey screamed.

'Come on ya big fat fool, wake up and check out the cave.'

He was in a state of total excitement about their discovery and showed little empathy to his mate's injuries. Harvey grabbed onto an overhanging branch and lowered himself into the opening. One foot found ground on Golly's back, the other on rock, his mate let out a groan.

'Oh, you are alive!'

Apart from his mate's suffering, Harvey could hear other movements in the cave and the occasional plonk of falling rocks as they hit water to his left. For a moment he feared the whole roof of the cave was going to collapse. There was also a sickly-sweet smell mixed with the smell of freshly disturbed soil in the air that was slightly masked by the cave's natural dank aroma. He lit a cigarette lighter which instantly showed the expanse of the cave. To his right on an adjacent ledge the movement came into focus. It was a carpet of writhing baby black snakes. Harvey stood paralysed with fear, unable to even scream, he was wondering where the mother was. Slowly one by one the snakes disappeared into cracks and fissures, but there was no sign of mum. The lighter burning his fingers bought Harvey back to reality, he jumped up on Golly's back and hauled himself out into the light.

By the time he had dusted himself off and parted with some of the fear of the snake encounter, Golly had also dragged himself out of the cave. Harvey looked over at his dishevelled mate and started laughing.

'You idiot Golly, you could have killed yourself!'

Goliath hardly offered a smile; he could barely talk. Apart from the cuts and scratches on his arms and legs that were now oozing blood through his dust and mud-covered skin, Goliath had a gaping hole in the base of his chin. A piece of rock or stick had skewered him in the fall.

'That's going to need a stitch or two Golly!'

Golly mumbled something back, but Harvey's thoughts now wandered elsewhere.

'Give us a hand to cover up our cave entry mate and we will go and see Aunty Trish about your damage.'

As usual, and despite his pain, Golly did what he was told. Together they dragged a couple of large rocks near the cave entry and broke off some tree branches and scrub to hide their new lair.

'Now remember mate this is our secret place, so don't go telling anyone ok!'

Golly nodded in agreement, but Harvey grabbed Golly's arm and rubbed it on his own scratched arm.

'We are Indian blood brothers now and bound by a secret code, ok, so when your chin heals the scar will be your star of courage and a reminder of our secret place. Do you know what I am on about Golly? It's our secret place till the sun comes up in the evening!'

Goliaths face brightened to a smile, as he mumbled a reply.

'Just like 'The Lone Ranger and Tonto' Harvey.'

Harvey smiled and felt a bit of pleasure at the power he had over his mate.

On their next visit they brought some torches and after checking no one was watching, they removed the branches and pushed the rocks to the side.

'You go first Golly, you found it.'

Golly fearlessly charged in through the dark opening.

'No snakes!' He yelled out, sensing his mate's hidden fear.

Harvey built up some courage and lowered himself down onto the landing rock. They sat there in the still damp cave for a moment with their torches on. Both were in a state of shock. The cavern, that had not seen light for a hundred years, suddenly came alive in a vivid tapestry of ancient ochre drawings of animals and hand stencils. Apart from the images of kangaroo, turtles, platypus and black and red hands, the most striking image of all was a rainbow painted eel that wound itself around the cave's inner walls and ceiling, where its body disappeared at one edge of the cave roof and reappeared on the other side about four metres away. The stunned boys were getting over their initial shock and scanned the length of the eel with their torches from the tip of its tail to its faded yellow head. They were startled at the way its razor-sharp band of teeth reflected in the torch light. It looked almost real, but the cold stare of the beast soon subdued their fear and at that moment both boys realised how unique their secret place was.

There was a sudden movement in the water on the floor of the cave and both torches focussed instantly on the same spot. They only caught a glimpse of what they disturbed, but they knew an eel tail when they saw one. Although they had only limited fishing experience at the lake, both had hooked eels before but never a 'power-pole' size giant. It would be months before they would work up the courage to go swimming again. But they kept that secret as well.

Over the next few years on school holidays and weekends they would visit their cave. Harvey never overcame his fear of snakes and always made Golly go first. Occasionally they would fish for the large eel from the roof of the cave. But gradually the large eel sighting faded from their memories, and they never saw it again.

Harvey knew their cave discovery was special and Golly, whose mental condition seemed to be getting worse, still went along with anything that Harvey suggested. Neither had any interest in Aboriginal culture but the clarity of the images and the eerie nature of the cave's stillness charged hidden senses in both boys. Although Harvey's evil selfish streak ran deep, he had developed a special bonding with his Golly Green mate. At times they would sit on the landing rock, torches in hand reflecting light from the colourful ceiling to the dark brooding water lapping at the white sandy beach below, both silent in peaceful thought.

Their time as children ended when the slow-moving river of childhood hit the rapids. Their adventures became less frequent as they grew further apart in maturity. They would always leave the cave entry secure, but they soon parted ways and the cave became a memory. Harvey fell in with some new acquaintances and learned some negative life skills like shop lifting and hot-wiring cars. His path ahead was set in concrete, while Goliath never changed.

Harvey came onto the local cop's radar in the late nineties when he had climbed up the criminal tree a little. They were only minor misdemeanours such as public nuisance and affray, but one officer, who took an interest in such wayward kids, sensed that this kid had a scarred attitude and a temper to match. Detective Harry Moffitt had a principle of putting foresight before hindsight and this had placed Harvey right up near the top of his watch list.

It was about two weeks after Sally Maitland's funeral

when her mum Jill made the discovery. She was going through Sally's things and at the back of the wardrobe, in the old black vinyl handbag she discovered a diary and some photos. Uncle Ray was arrested that week.

Apparently, in his words, he just picked the 'weakest of the litter' for his depraved photography and sexual gratification. Harvey had sensed it; Jess and Jill did not have a clue and poor Sally had worn the brunt of his evil. Aunty Trish gave back via charity for the rest of her life, serving the local street urchins at soup kitchens around Parramatta. Jill went back to St John of God for a spell and Jess moved interstate with her boyfriend. When Harvey was interviewed by the Police about the incident his statement read,

'Yeah, life sucks and then you die, so move on.'

Moffitt was not surprised.

Harvey's life floated awkwardly down the river of petty crime and odd jobs. He shunned relationships and never really had any respect for women. Occasionally he dated but purely for sexual gratification. Eventually he met an obliging soul who he could possess. Her name was Sandy Cooper, she was a pretty girl with an overwhelming need for a controlling partner. Strangely, some women who come from violent family settings are attracted to the very thing they tried to escape from. In Sandy's case it was her father. Since the age of twelve he had shown her an inappropriate amount of attention that finally led to violence and rape. She was too scared to fight and too withdrawn to report it. The abuse went on for four years until she escaped with a girlfriend and fled to Kings Cross. She was well on the way to a life of drugs and prostitution when she met Harvey.

It was a chance meeting at Burwood railway station. Harvey was dealing small quantities of pot and Sandy was in obvious need. He was instantly taken in by her figure and face. She was empathetic to the story of his sister Sally and thought she understood his inconsistent ways. Their relationship lasted four years in total with sporadic break-ups. Continual bruising and the black eyes caused their first split. This soon became a monthly event, but Sandy kept returning for more. She always forgave him and made excuses for her condition and his violence. Eventually a girlfriend with fortitude entered the scene and helped her execute an apprehended violence order. It was to be one of many. Harvey was not one for being told what to do especially by the law and persisted with contact. Occasionally he managed to get Sandy back for a day or two, but after sex, another bashing and a call to the police, the drama of escape was repeated.

Thankfully, a women's refuge group became involved and moved Sandy to a new location. This was to be the last time Harvey saw her.

'I gave the ungrateful witch everything.' He was heard to say.

A female Police officer replied,

'Yes, including the scars!'

CHAPTER 6

Lake Life

Anne sat on the edge of the hot tub and stared out through the rain speckled plate glass window of the Spa room at the Crown Plaza. The mixed weather had not succeeded in dampening her will to enjoy a romantic weekend with Jake if anything it enhanced it. A warm smell of salt, perfume and body odour twitched her nose as she watched two droplets of water meander down the pane, to become one together at the end of their journey. Just like the droplets, Jake, and Anne both had long journeys before meeting again in the autumn of their two eventful lives.

Jake laid back in the bubbling hot water soaking in the ambience, watching her. To him she looked like a sculpture of a Roman goddess. Over the sound of bubbles and water jets he tried to capture her attention.

'Where are you, Miss Anne?' He called, reminiscing on the name he called her when they had first met on a school swimming day at the Parramatta pool in 1966.

'Nowhere special Jake, I was just thinking.'

'I told you to leave your mother at home and think of yourself this weekend.'

'I know Jake, it's just when I see the ocean, I remember the happy times mum had at Pottsville during the Christmas holidays, when we were kids.'

'Well, this is Terrigal, half a lifetime later and I'm here with my hot tempting lover, who needs to have some fun. So, let us party!'

'I think I would prefer a night of romance and perhaps a dance.' She smirked.

'That's my girl, we may as well throw in a bottle of Moet and make it an unforgettable weekend.'

'That's got my vote Jake.'

Anne shuffled closer and wrapped her legs around his. The warmth of Jake's smile said it all.

The weekend away had been a restful escape. Anne was now more determined to push on and come to terms with her mother's problems. As for Jake, he had his own mounting family dramas to contend with. His daughter Lisa had gone through hell after she presented Jake with a granddaughter. She named her Layla, after the song of the same name. It was always a grand feeling for Jake to hold a baby again and to relive all the happy moments from his past, but in Layla's case there was a medical problem. The anxiety of a pending operation to remove a brain tumour, wrestled with the optimism shown by the doctors. It was a matter of wait and see, while the whole family suffered heart ache.

Jake's son Stan and his wife Lidia now had four children, the last a boy was proudly named Jacob. The whole family was growing fast and with it the mushroom cloud of dramas and decisions. Life always seemed to get more complicated, but the giving and getting of love from all Jake's children and grandchildren made it all worthwhile.

The following Saturday, after a busy morning, Jake set out on an afternoon lake circuit walk, determined not to think about all the family troubles. He started to relate to his senses and keep his deeper thoughts under control. He was seeing letter boxes, houses, sculptured gardens, road signs and traffic lights. He was hearing horns blaring, brakes squealing, children laughing, dogs barking and the constant din of cicadas. He could smell curry's cooking, chops burning, fragrant gardenias and the diesel fumes from passing trucks. It was of no use, he put his immediate family dramas to one side for a moment and his mind went back onto Anne's mother and all her problems.

When they awoke earlier on that morning, enshrined in the days humidity, Jake's first thought was to go for a swim. Anne had a different agenda in store. He was generally submissive and caring to her needs and could tell by the sadness in her soft morning smile that she was on a low despite the previous weekend of fun.

Anne, like Jake had a dysfunctional upbringing. Her father was a hard worker but a low earner. He had a home brew fuelled temper and a fistful of excuses to lose it. Love, like presents was in short supply and generally second hand. She had always thought that her mother Judy hated her and her sisters, within the constant battle to win his attention. His girls were his property and in later life when they started dating boys, his abuse and control gradually severed all family bonds. Judy was left quivering and often, literally hid in a wardrobe. Like all good family 'closet skeletons', pain faded with age. After their dads suffering death to asbestos cancer, Judy's fragile mind began to deteriorate.

The old house became a shrine to the husband she wished she had, and memories of a few good times became epic stories of devotion. All the bad memories the daughters had, kept the family scattered, both mentally and physically. With no concept as to the extent of Judy's mental demise over the years, apart from occasional phone calls and neighbour reports. Anne felt compelled to re-enter her mother's life. Initially Anne was amazed at the state of Judy's house and garden but after her and Jake straightened a few things up, lopped their way through the privet bush to the front door, and cleaned the house to its prior lived-in glory, they managed to bring some stability and sustenance back into Judy's life, at least for a brief time. A high-risk dementia ward was just around the corner.

To Jake the morning had felt like a waste of pleasant weather. His plans for a swim and an afternoon hike at Lake Parramatta had been partly ruined. Anne's mother required an assessment at the Hospital for cataract eye surgery. This meant a pickup from the nursing home, three hours of short conversations and waiting. His involvement was to drive, support and keep up the supply of tea and muffins during the ordeal of hospital forms and smiling matrons. He secretly thought that 'time wasting' was a post graduate course for public professionals.

The excreta and urine stench clung to the follicles of Anne's nose as she entered her mum's room at the Nursing home. She cleaned her mother and helped her change her soiled underwear, while Jake waited in the car. A nurse would generally take care of this whole exercise, but Anne felt compelled to do it. She had an unwarranted feeling of guilt. The placement of her mother into a nursing home had been a daunting exercise. Despite Jake's support, external family members were throwing in some abuse peppered with little understanding of Judy's accelerating dementia.

It was mid-afternoon by the time they got home from the hospital. While Anne got stuck into some housework, Jake saw his chance and took off for a bush walk around the Lake Parramatta circuit. His pace quickened and his troubled thoughts subsided. As he walked on in rhythm to his knees clicking like castanets, the thought of future titanium kneecaps was also worth leaving behind. Being fifty plus in body and twenty plus in mind was hard to reconcile. The smell of a wet eucalypts and burnt wood, told him he had just missed a drenching. The forecast was for a fine day with scattered afternoon showers, so far, his luck was holding out.

He left the fire trail and headed down towards the creek where old car wrecks stood like iconic reminders to a bygone era. An old green, now rusted panel van, spoke of hooning about and 'shaggin' wagons' of the seventies. Jake recalled parking down at the lake with his girlfriend's following the late-night fright flicks at the Blacktown drive-in theatre, back in the good old days when youth held superhuman strength and could deflect bullets. Other vehicles included a burnt out P76, 'a mini cooper's mother' so named due to its humongous boot.

Recollections of Whitlam, 'It's Time' and just missing out on the Vietnam War, flooded Jake's mind with 'what might have been' scenarios. Jake and an old scout mate Ken were the only two in their group to have their birthday ballot ball drop. Their mothers had kittens and their girlfriends shed tears. They went through all the paperwork and health checks prior to basic training, then good old Gough and the Labour Party got elected and canned the call up, empathy faded to a warm 'what could have been status.' Life is always full of variants.

A fairy wren with a chestnut brown body and a flash of turquoise on its head caught Jake's attention. As he stopped for a better look, he snagged his foot on a length of fishing line, carelessly left across the path. At that moment, above the dank smell of the freshwater lake, there was a whiff of something dead in the adjacent damp leaf litter. Jake followed the line hand over hand over a gnarled root of a fallen tree. At first glance he thought what he saw was a human arm, on closer inspection he realised it was the snake-shaped body and pointed head of a long dead eel. As he quickly walked off and away from the stench an amusing memory crossed his mind.

Some years earlier in a previous relationship, his girlfriend's eldest boy Dirk was fined for illegal trout fishing in the back waters of Warragamba Dam. Occasionally, on Sunday afternoons Dirk would bring home a couple of large rainbow trout. After being scolded and lectured on the possibility of fines, the fish were cleaned and quickly disposed of in a succulent feast. The ranger spotted Dirk and his mate just as Dirk landed a big one. The ranger gave chase as the boys bolted for freedom; they had no intention of getting caught. Dirk's mate had the smarts to leave his gear, but Dirk took off with the rod in tow and fish dragging behind. Naturally, the fish got snagged and the line was running out at a rate of knots, when it reached the end of the spool the rod was jerked out of his hand. At this stage Dirk thought he was in the clear and hid behind a huge ghost gum. As a kookaburra laughed in the distance, the ranger followed the line hand over hand, reached around the tree and grabbed Dirk by the scruff of the neck. The fine was substantial, but he got to keep the fish.

A specialist doctor once told them that Dirk was a strange lad. Tests revealed he had ADHD and he fluctuated between an Einstein and Forrest Gump in IQ. This manifested itself in many ways. Jake had once questioned if Dirk had fixed his car's punctured tyre, the bemused look meant no. So, the next hour was spent looking for the wheel that Dirk had ditched after changing the spare.

A goanna strolled past and the din of cockatoo's protecting their eggs brought Jake's attention back to the walk. He was now on the final leg of the hike and the plan was for a coffee at Mary's Café. This would be followed by a BBQ with Anne at home and a good movie. He looked up and across the lake saw Billy the butcher at his favourite spot on the old watch tower platform.

Seventy years back this area was western Sydney's beach and weekends bought kids and family's by the hundreds to swim, dive and fish in water that was reasonably clean. It was so popular that it boasted Australia's largest freshwater Life Saving club. So called progress and development of surrounding subdivisions, finally led to its closure. Environment was not a big-ticket item back in the seventies and sewage, pesticides and illegal dumping finally led to its closure on public risk grounds. Only in recent years had its quality improved enough to risk eating the lake's inhabitants and taking an occasional swim.

None of this seemed to bother Billy Chan, he often took what he caught home for one of his Chinese culinary creations.

Every fisherman has one, the one that got away, big one, the beast or just my old mate down yonder. Billy did not beat around the bush when talking about his giant. Its tag was Elvis, and he was the King, a fish, a fresh-water eel. Elvis had a snake-shaped body of about three metres long and he was close to a metre in girth after a feed. His bulbous eyes and large pectoral fins helped him navigate along the lake bottom in search of food. Elvis unlike the other smaller finned eels in the lake had a distinctive yellow saddle on his back and stomach. It gave him a certain regal appearance. This was his lake and he let Billy know it. He could cause the fishing line to sing in the wind and create whirlpools of black mud as he danced around the bottom of the lake. A lake named in his honour 'Parramatta' from the Aboriginal Burramatta. Burra for food or eel, Matta for place, or the place where Eels lie down to rest.

Billy sang his stories. He didn't have a 'wooden heart' when he told people with 'suspicious minds', that his beast was the 'devil in disguise'. His 'hound dog' smirk gave way to his sarcastic wit that always led to his close encounter yarns. Such as the day Elvis raised his long yellow breasted body out of the water and told Billy that if he ever caught him, he had to 'love him tender' and let him go. There were times when Billy would have done just that. But on other occasions, when Billy was not quite himself, he may have chosen to cook him tender and cook him slow.

About sixty years after Arthur Phillip and some British

sailors rowed up the river from Farm Cove and founded a settlement at Rose Hill, the Chun clan found their way to the growing town called Parramatta. Billy's family lines were all blessed with a genetic disposition to wealth creation, through arduous work and Chinese luck. The Chinese and British opium wars of the 1840's gave Bill's ancestor Wei Chun a foothold in the colony. Somehow, he held on through years of oppression and racist hate. The local currency lads and editorials gave all the Chinese workers a tough time. This was even though the gentry who shipped the Chinese in, thought the Orientals work ethos was far superior.

As time went on, they kept to themselves and thrived in an environment where prostitution and opium dens provided back up funds for legitimate business such as gold prospecting or growing fruit and vegetables. In the Parramatta area these market gardens could be found on the alluvial soils adjacent to the tributary creeks of the main river. As the new 'China-towns' ebbed and flowed within the forces of bigotry, the Chun name changed to the more locally acceptable Anglican name of Chaney. This lasted up until Bill's great grandfather called himself William Chan. The whole family found their talents in the food industry. In Billy's case it was butcher shops.

Billy Chan considered himself a true Australian. He blended well into the multi-cultural Parramatta, with his Cantonese looks and Aussie accent. He had built up a thriving butcher business on the North Rocks Road and his special award-winning sausages were the popular choice of all his customers. Bill spent his quiet times fishing for eels in the best spot at Lake Parramatta, the old jetty in front of Mary's Café. He often donated free meat to the local senior citizens and charity days. Everyone seemed to like him.

Every other Friday night, down at the Rose and Thorn Hotel, when the karaoke was in full swing, Bill could be found showing off his other talent as an Elvis Presley impersonator. He was considered a real talent by the locals. He would waddle up to the mike in his skin-tight white sequinned suit, to swags of woof whistles. Then with a wide toothy smile and a wind-milling arm, he started his song with the trademark 'thank you very much' in a voice as deep as he could muster. The crowd went wild, and happiness boiled.

The only person who was not happy with Bill was his wife, Susan. She was constantly nagging him about house chores that he never got done. Bill's busy lifestyle was running in the opposite direction to his wife's needs and Bill knew it.

'G'day Bill, any luck with Elvis today?' asked Jake.

Billy had his secrets and his worries but never was he seen without his trademark welcome grin.

'G'day Jake, no mate, the big fella is having a snooze somewhere up stream in the reed beds, dreaming of his next meal.'

'Either that or planning his escape over that dam wall, Bill.'

'Elvis is too big and lazy for that now Jake. A thousand-kilometre swim for one last fling has faded from his body clock.'

'How old do you reckon he is Bill?'

'I'd say at least a hundred years, he probably made his way up the river before they put that concrete capping on top of the dam wall.'

'Did you lose one recently Bill?'

'What do you mean Jake?'

Jake became aware of a slight change in Bill's mood.

'I saw and smelt a dead eel up by the overhang cave just now. He still has the gear and line attached. I thought you may be losing your knack.'

'No, not one of mine Jake, I haven't fished that end of the lake for years.'

Over his shoulder Jake saw that Fritz was having his afternoon coffee at Mary's Café, so he wished Bill good luck and continued his walk to the café.

He was still thinking about Bill's mood change when Fritz greeted him as he came up the steps.

'What did you say to upset China, Jake?'

Jake turned to see Bill packing up his gear and heading off.

'Nothing, other than mentioning I found a dead eel. I suspect Bill doesn't like other people fishing in his lake.'

'You're probably right Jake, that china-man is too weird for my liking.'

One thing Jake hated in people was subtle racism and although Fritz was a regular acquaintance, Jake bounced on the comment.

'That so called china-man is more Australian than you Fritz, and his name is Bill!'

Fritz saw the annoyance in Jake's face and quickly changed the subject.

'I heard Anne has organised a school re-union here at the Café in a couple of weeks, for the 'Arthur Phillip High'

Baby Boomers.'

'I'm glad you didn't say old farts Fritz, but you're right and Mary says that you're going to be our security chief on the night.'

'That's ok by me Jake, I'm not one for getting drunk while listening to old timers going on about their ailments. It's better to sit back, watch and laugh.'

'You may have a point Fritz.'

Fritz Kruger was caretaker of the park. To most of his acquaintances he was just a grumble bum. His Germanic origin was made obvious by his height, blonde hair, blue eyes, and sharp controlled conversations. His father Klaus was one of Hitler's Aryan youth troops, who often bragged about shaking hands with the Fuehrer, at a presentation of local civic medals in Ulm in 1938. At the wars end, he went on to work for the local state-owned power company, on a poverty income. Fritz's family managed to emigrate in the early fifties. In a strange set of circumstances, Klaus was billed by the Government for the sum one thousand nine hundred marks following an accident. In Klaus's mind the fact that he was coming home from work at the time of the fall, entitled him to full compensation. Despite repeated requests and an ongoing bureaucratic letter procession, they started to deduct the funds from his dismal salary.

A month after the family left Germany there was a local police investigation into a grand theft. On a cold snow-clad winter night, a redundant high voltage cable that crossed the river, was cut away and stolen. The Police Inspector in charge of the investigation believed it had to be the work of a professional gang. Further investigations, later, led to the arrest of a scrap metal dealer who revealed that although the goods value was more than five thousand marks, the thief was adamant that he should receive exactly one thousand nine hundred marks in cash.

Fritz was a worker and his father always said that there were only two types of people in the world, 'Workers or Farmers'. In later years when business took Fritz to Germany in a time before the 'Wall' came down, he got pleasure and a tad of trouble by calling the East German communist border guards 'Farmers'. He had a knack for treading on the wrong toes. A great deal of life lessons is gained from our parents and to this end Fritz was no exception. He was frugal without being mean and had a withdrawn personality, always maintaining a cautious presence with strangers, especially non-Caucasian types. He often recalled the story of his father's first job interview, after their arrival in Sydney. Knowing only a few English words he thought it best to meet and befriend some of the locals at the nearest hotel. An introduction letter had been given to him by the clerk at the Immigration Office, for a job interview at the local Supply Authority.

He was deeply knowledgeable in his electrical profession and aspired to be part of this growth industry in a post war Australia. He met a fellow named Jack Carter, who eventually became a lifelong friend. Jack was your typical Aussie larrikin and saw an opportunity to have a laugh at Klaus's expense by tutoring him with some Aussie colloquial expressions to be used at the interview.

Klaus felt well-rehearsed on the day of his interview and with a confident smile told the Personnel Officer that he would gladly take his 'bloody job' and offered to take him out for 'a piss-up at the Pub'. The interview finished with

Klaus telling the interviewer he was 'a good old-bugger' and he would work 'his guts out in an Iron lung'. Obviously, the Personnel Officer saw through the language barrier because Klaus went on to a successful career in the power industry. He had also learnt a great Australian lesson on how to avoid gullibility traps.

Fritz left school in 1967. He had a few girlfriends but considered himself not the marrying kind. He had a wandering spirit and never settled down to a career or steady job. By the year 1994 he had been all over the world working in various occupations from oil rig work to a merchant seaman. At one stage he even had a sales management role in Europe. He returned home to Australia in 1995 deciding to settle down and pursue a more relaxed bachelor lifestyle. With luck he secured a job with the council as caretaker at Lake Parramatta. It was a live on-site job and a perfect spot to quell his wandering spirit.

Fritz's sister Mary was looking to start a business around the time he settled into the new job. As luck would have it the lake Café lease was available, and Mary jumped at the opportunity to give it a go. She was extraordinarily successful. Over the following year the business flourished. It seems the locals appreciated the coffee, food, and views. Regular patrons such as local schoolteachers and chat groups had to reserve tables due to its popularity. The smile on Mary's face said it all. Despite the demanding work life was good.

'Good afternoon Jake, will it be the usual?'

'Thanks Mary.'

She was head down and flushed faced, cleaning up after a late lunch crowd, but she still found time to get Jake a cappuccino and have a quick chat.

Mary was a stepsister to Fritz and was born on an Alice Springs Mission in 1956. She was adopted by her German parents in part as a debt of gratitude to the new country that had welcomed them and offered so much. They raised and loved her as part of the family in an untroubled home. From 1910 to 1970 Aboriginal children, full blood, and those of mixed descent, were forcibly removed from their families and placed in state institutions, church missions, or white families for foster or adoption. Those who were removed in this way later became known as the Stolen Generation. Mary was told of her adoption when she was ten. She loved her parents deeply but longed to know of her culture and history. She was very artistic as a child and there were some very strange and mystic experiences as she grew.

Fritz, who was two years older, knew his sister was special. He had witnessed her in a trance like state on several occasions, when they were young children. At times she would sit upright in bed, still deep in sleep and chant in a strange language. At first her parents were concerned by this and had Mary checked out by various specialists. They all gave her a clean bill of health and told Klaus that it was just a passing phase. As time went on the mystic chants waned. Mary went on to become an accomplished artist. She never made a great deal of money from it, but her life was whole.

In the late eighties she tracked down her Aboriginal relatives, and although upset that her biological parents had died, she was heartened to discover that her family tree consisted of 'Story tellers', the Shaman of her clan. Her mother was a full blood member of the Arrernte people and her father a Scottish drover from an outback station. The mysticism of her youth had had a dreamtime footing. This together with the recent 'Government Sorry Day' conclusion to past policy errors, gave Mary a sense of place in both worlds.

'Would you like something to eat Jake?'

'No thanks Mary, I'll be off now, I'm cooking a BBQ tonight and I don't want Anne to send out a search party. By the way how are the plans going for the school reunion dinner?'

'It's all arranged and looks like the numbers are in at fifty, which surprised me. I thought a lot of the class of '69 would have moved on to greener pastures by now.'

'Yeah, well it will be good to see how time has dealt its cards, eh Mary.'

'That's right Jake, most of you white fella's grey early!' She said with a smirk.

'White fella's Mary? If my old memory serves me correctly Arthur Phillip High carried the flags of all Nations. You might be closer to the mark saying rainbow fella's.'

'Good point Jake, catch you later.'

CHAPTER 7

Goliath Maitland

The river of time flows fast for most people, but for some handicapped people like Goliath Maitland it can slow to a trickle.

In the year 1821 the Female Factory at Parramatta was first occupied. It was commissioned by Governor Macquarie in 1818 and designed by convict architect Francis Greenway. Originally it was intended as a place of refuge and punishment for convict women and their children, but it soon became a purgatory on earth. Designed to accommodate three hundred, the Factory's female population peaked at 1203 and 263 children in 1842.

The Female Factory complex contained a three-story central dormitory and a mess building. Extensive out buildings, gardens and solitary cells were also enclosed within a high perimeter wall. The flow of convicts to NSW ended in 1840 and in 1848 it was proclaimed an Asylum for Lunatic and Invalid Convicts. With the ghosts of its sad history, it lives on today as part of the Cumberland Area Psychiatric Health District and only the walls remain as a monument to the pain and suffering of those poor wretches.

Some of the old outbuildings and dormitories built later in the nineteenth century are today home to rehabilitation units and drug clinics. Other buildings, like Carnation Cottage, house mid-range mentally handicapped inmates. These unfortunates are not bad enough to be kept under lock and key but are not capable of living in general society. Goliath was one such case. For the past twenty-eight years since his parents were forced to give him up, he had lived in a garden room off the porch of the Carnation cottage. Although secured by a large fence and gate it offered Goliath and fellow inmates a degree of sanctuary and peace. This meant that in some cases conditional control medications could be reduced.

A convict-built sandstone wall that was part of the original female factory was now the backdrop of a courtyard adjacent to Goliath's garden room. From here you could hear the rapid water of the Parramatta River, crossing the rocks as it approached the weir at 'Little Coogee'. You could also hear and smell the fruit bat colony, where the flying foxes hung like socks on a clothesline from the ghost gums by the riverbank. This was all a stone's throw from Goliath's garden where a grand grapefruit tree stood.

It was a tree of power within the middle of a soft green lawn, surrounded by Australian native shrubs. When Goliath was first brought to this place it was half his size. While it grew, he grew. The tree now was five metres in girth and Goliath was two metres tall, they were both giants of their own nature. Within Goliath's mind a connection had been made with the tree. It became a measure of an unknown need within him, its fruits of life and seasonal changes somehow blended with his needs. Once when a storm partially damaged a branch of the tree Goliath became aggressive with one of his carers. His medication was increased for a time, but the reason went undetected. He would often lie for hours at the tree base, looking up through its green branches. The filtered sunlight, blue sky and white clouds were a coloured canvas background to a three-dimensional image of bright yellow orbs of fruit and vivid green leaves. He would lay there staring almost willing the fruit to fall.

Each day blended into the next, weeks into months and months into years. The grapefruit tree grew strong, and its fruit was plentiful. Recent summer storms caused it no harm and Goliath was calm. 'The Golly Green Giant' was still within him. Despite the intervening years and few visits from his mum, Goliath remembered the brief time that 'Harvey Hate' spent with them like it was yesterday. It was his day-in-the-sun of a life with minor change. On the outside he was a 180 kg man, on the inside he was still that boy. There were people in the Cottage that treated him well and over time they became his family. His roommate for the last few years was a quiet fellow named Vince. Opposite in stature and nature, Vince never showed an interest in anything. These days to Goliath he was just another item of furniture.

The Head Psychiatrist was made aware of Goliath's consistent good behaviour and suggested a little more freedom could do no harm. At first one of the carers escorted both Vince and Goliath on local daytime walks and even on occasions a local bushwalk around Lake Parramatta reserve. As time went on and their good behaviour remained constant, their freedom was increased in stages.

Eventually they were allowed out by themselves for morning walks on condition that they return for lunch.

Vince did not always accompany Goliath, most of the time they did their own thing. While walking around the institution grounds Goliath began to help a little. Sometimes he might assist maintenance workers by digging a trench or help delivery drivers unload a truck. His behaviour was rewarded and recorded, but on sunny afternoons you could always find him lying under that big old grapefruit tree, staring skywards.

Harvey had moved back home after breaking up with Sandy, that was to last a year. His mother tried but deep down she knew her son was trouble. She longed for a quiet life and so arranged for him to live with his Uncle Pat in Parramatta. It was not much of a joint, but he had a dry room, and he could come and go as he pleased. Pat had not changed, he was still a dirty old hermit, mostly drunk and as sneaky as ever. Harvey had scored for himself part-time work that payed cash for delivering stationary, print cartridges and software for a legit business mate of his mothers. This gave him a good supplement to his Centre-link cheque and a reason for being seen here and there around town. Stationary deliveries were easy on the back, and this blended well with his lazy attitude.

His mind was all over the place as he pulled up at the Cumberland Gatehouse. The morning just got busier. Rick had rung about an urgent delivery to one of his best customers. The clandestine nature of these calls amused him. Rick's message was short and to the point.

'Our man at the Bank needs twelve cartons of A4.'

The code for cocaine in criminal circles was generally an ounce or an eight ball, but due to phone taps and such,

Rick always used other wording with different agents. In Harvey's case this worked in with his new front job, an ounce was a carton of A4, and an eight-ball was a carton of A3. The number 12 in this case meant a noon delivery. Money never changed hands. Rick had other ways to receive payment. He rarely had problems as most clients knew of his reputation.

Harvey was only aware of his part of the business. He would pick up the pack from his stash and deliver it. In this case 'Stan the Man'. Stan Burke was a regular at the Woolpack Hotel in George Street. It had the reputation as holding the longest license of any other drinking establishment in Australia. The meeting location was 'The Hanging Wall' at the rear of the Commonwealth Bank. This was an appropriate place to conduct a criminal transaction. The convict-built sandstone wall was once part of the original Court house and Police station that was built in 1839. What made this particular cell wall famous were the number of murderers and thieves that were hung there in Australia's harsh beginnings.

It was 9:00am. That gave Harvey just three hours to complete his deliveries, pick up an A4 from his stash and get to the wall. The day had suddenly turned busy. As he drove past the gate house off Fleet Street a dopey big bloke walked in front of his ute. Harvey had to brake with a skid that scared both himself and the pedestrian. As they eyeballed one another the big bloke placed both his hands on the bonnet of the car and stared at Harvey with a 'Cheshire Cat' grin.

In Goliath's mind it was only yesterday that he and 'Harvey Hate' knocked around together and although Harvey was now thirty years older, to Goliath he had not changed a bit. Harvey on the other hand screamed out of the car window,

'Get ya hands off the car ya bloody idiot!'

Goliath gave him a glib hurtful look and bewildered by Harvey's sharp response replied,

'Harvey Hate' and 'The Golly Green Giant' ride again, Hi Ho Silver away!'

Harvey's jaw dropped as he realised who it was.

'Golly, ya fat fool I thought you were dead.'

Goliath was so pleased to see him that as Harvey got out of the car, he grabbed him in a bear hug, almost crushing him with happiness. Harvey could not believe his old mates strength. Straight away Harvey was thinking of ways he could use his long lost and more importantly strong mate.

They exchanged some idle chatter, but it did not take long for Harvey to realise they were miles apart in maturity and smarts. Goliath spoke about his world with limited language, his garden, his friend Vince, the good helpers in Carnation cottage and his lake walks. The latter got Harvey's attention, for a minute he thought that Goliath may still remember the location of the cave they found. Harvey had recently rediscovered their childhood retreat and to his surprise it had remained undiscovered by the general public. The entry point was well concealed by scrub and fallen trees and the large rock that he and Goliath had rolled into place was still there. Over the last year Harvey had made several visits to the site and fitted the cave out with some storage bins and battery lighting. It had become a true underground lair of a Super Villain. He stored his drug stash and other stolen property there in complete secrecy.

As Goliath helped unload the Ute, Harvey's mind was racing with ways he could use his strong dopey mate. One way would be to help secure the cave site. This was made easier by Goliath's newfound freedom. He would also come in handy as a bit of back-up muscle if the need ever arose. Harvey knew his old mate would do anything to protect him. He was also aware of the control drugs that Goliath would be on to keep him calm. If Harvey could manage this area, he could effectively bring back the mad ass Golly of old when and if required.

'Golly old mate I have to go now, but I'll come back on Tuesday. We will go and do some exploring around the lake eh!'

'Yeah, Harvey we could check out our Pirate cave too!'

'Your memory is surprisingly good Golly?'

'Yeah, I remember the fun we had there, and it all comes back when I look in the mirror to shave in the morning before Vince and I go to breakfast, see Harvey.'

Goliath was pointing to a perfect star scar on the underside of his chin.

'Remember Harvey, you called it my star of courage.'

'Oh, that's right mate, tell me do you remember telling anybody else about the cave?'

'Course not Harvey, we made an Indian blood pact just like 'The Lone Ranger' and 'Tonto', don't ya remember Harvey?'

'Yeah, mate it comes back to me now, don't forget we're still blood brothers Golly and our secrets still stand.'

'Yeah mate, till the sun comes up in the evening!' Goliath

laughed.

Harvey could not get over some of Goliaths crystal memories, it gave him an unusual feeling of bonding to another human. Something that Harvey had gone without for most of his life.

'Ok Golly see ya next Tuesday morning just up from the gate house. We'll check out the cave eh mate?'

'Swell Harvey, see ya then eh!'

As Harvey drove off the big fella smiled like all his Christmas's came at once. He turned into Fleet Street and the baffled sound of 'Hi Ho Silver away' faded into the background. It lingered on for a time somewhere deep within Harvey, at a place he rarely visited nor knew much about. With his smile still in place Goliath retreated to his tree of peace, it had been his happiest day in thirty years.

CHAPTER 8

Muhammad (Marvin) Khan

It was late September in 1980 and the 11th month of the Muslim lunar calendar, when the opportunity of escape was offered to the war wearied Khan Family. Muhammad Khan, along with his parents had no choice but to seek out a new land of peace. Academics were cannon fodder for both sides in this war. The annual Hajj pilgrimage offered their best chance. Muhammad's father Haseeb had wanted to attend the Hajj for most of his adult life. Millions of other Muslim pilgrims made this dangerous annual journey to the Muslim holy cities of Mecca and Medina every year. Followers of Islam are required by their faith to try and make the pilgrimage at least once in their lifetime. This act of faith would serve two purposes for the Khan family. Not, just for their religious belief, but for their survival as well.

The cold winds of the Hindu Kush rushed through the open windows of the ancient bus and stung the eyes of the distraught travellers. They were fleeing from the Russian invaders, who offered less freedom than the previous Mujahidin warlords. This exodus was all about survival.

Kabul to Islamabad was only five hundred kilometres via the Khyber Pass, but it was the most treacherous route in the world. The group of twenty had only been robbed once since entering the pass. They were surviving on their own defences with will power, wit and knives as their only back up. The old bus, resplendent in the cultural Pakistani baubles and trinkets, was constantly over heating in the mountainous terrain. In times of peace this trip would have only taken eight hours. But as they approached the notional safety of the Pakistan border crossing, they had been traveling on safer back roads for near ten hours and their spirits were low.

It was early morning and the Russian border guards had not hit the vodka yet when the bus pulled up at the crossing. The captain checked out all the papers and peered, with obvious lust, at the eyes of the Burka wearing women. The captain was no fool. He knew how a Mujahidin warrior would react. There were none on this bus, but he still had all the men stand out in the freezing wind for an hour. They were thoroughly searched and robbed of most of their meagre possessions. Luckily, the women held onto the most valuable items. Fear flowed through the bus like a thick mud slide, but their faith won out and finally the bus was waved on through. There was the light of hope at the end of the tunnel. Six months later and after Haseeb had trekked to Mecca for the Hajj, Muhammad Khan and his family sailed into Port Phillip Bay Melbourne.

Back in the 1860s Afghan cameleers came to Australia. For fifty years they were crucial in the exploration and development of the Australian outback by carrying supplies across the vast continent. Their fearless determination won them acclaim throughout the nation. Today the

Adelaide to Darwin train 'The Ghan' is a legacy named in their honour. It was also an honour for Muhammad Khan and his family to be allowed refugee status in Australia following the dreaded Soviet occupation of their homeland. They too showed a fearless determination in the exodus from their war-torn land. Their journey was fraught with danger, but the rights to cultural maintenance and social justice that Australia offered was like a magnet to all the terrified refugees. Muhammad loved his homeland but was fearful for its future. In Australia there was hope, peace and above all freedom.

Muhammad was well educated and had previously taught languages at Kabul University. Apart from his skills as a teacher, he had also published a book of poems and short stories about life and death in a tribal society. Always a loner, he found it hard to settle into the multicultural Melbourne environment. His parents had established a small grocery business in Braybrook a northern suburb. While the only work he could get was unskilled. He longed to teach again, but that would mean more study. Recognition of his skills in this new land was always going to be a challenge.

It was on a sizzling summer's day, with a hot northwest wind blowing, when Muhammad's life veered off in a new direction. His parents had taken the old van down to West Footscray to pick up some stock. It was a special anniversary day. It had been exactly five years to the day that they had moved to Australia. As usual Haseeb was having trouble negotiating Melbourne's traffic mayhem. An incident of road rage at traffic lights in Ashley Street had caused his good mood to change. His concentration lapsed for just a moment as he turned left into Sredna street from the busy Sunshine Road. It was a one-way street. Their van had a head on with a semi-trailer, carrying of all things grocery items. Both Haseeb and his wife were killed instantly.

Depression hit Muhammad hard for a while. The Sunshine Road and Sredna street intersection became a shrine that he visited daily. He would stand there for an hour or more, just thinking and praying for his parents. Real sunshine had left his life.

One cold, wet, and miserable Melbourne day Muhammad awoke with a life changing decision. He would change his name and move to Sydney. Two months later he rented a unit in Parramatta and made a fresh start as Marvin Khan.

He was still finding it difficult to get a work in the education sector and would have to rely on odd jobs to get by. Lady luck was with him when he ran into Bob Stickles one day, while browsing at Stickles Emporium for furniture in his unit. Bob was a good judge of character and liked Marvin from the start. After phoning around, he found him some local part time work. Later, he introduced him to lots of new acquaintances, like Jake and Steve, but life for Marvin was never easy. He felt isolated in time and had a need to express himself amid a speeding society. To this end, he came up with the concept of casting a message of hope to help him mentally escape his island of solitude.

To a psychologist, Marvin would have been analysed as a deep thinker, not as some would say, a manic depressive. He chose a modern vessel for his 'message in a bottle', a computer disk. He included all his previous life writings and a recent story of his family's struggles and trauma. He then burnt the disk with all his pent-up feelings of guilt, hope, wonder and ambitions. All of this was written in his new language, English. He then vacuums sealed it in an indestructible coffin of plastic and securely fixed it with lead sinkers to keep it on the floor of its watery time capsule. His hope was that in some future age the crumbling dam wall would give way to gravity's will and expose his story to a more enlightened culture. This would include the remnants of our materialistic past such as shopping trolleys, car bodies and other human junk. To this end, he set forth on his daily walk to the Lake Reserve, as today's custodian of loneliness in a mad world. Deep inside, he felt like a lonely raindrop on a dry rock, with his spirit being absorbed by hard surroundings.

Marvin rounded the bend into View St and headed on down to the lake. He thought about the contrast of life in the city and a walk in the bush. It occurred to him that the bush never seemed to age, it was always the same. In his eyes even the road signs looked tired. It is only humans and their designs that seem to suffer from the degradation of time. His thoughts then drifted back to last month's events and his run in at Centre-link with Harvey Maitland.

The only thing cool about Harvey was his name, and perhaps his inner-city glad rags. Older people sniggered at the modern Pirate getup, but for some reason, young woman in tight fitting miniskirts could not take their eyes off him. Apart from that, the rest of him added up to a 1.6 metre, ninety kilos bag of pure evil. He bragged about cruelty to cats and had a cane toad's share of empathy for everything else in the living world. Marvin had heard the town gossip from some of his new mates, about Harvey's treatment of Sandy. Bob also told him that he once treated his own Mum like an unwanted house servant and that as a kid his two sisters were punching bags. He was the sort of bloke you tried to avoid at all costs, but Marvin only saw the good in people. He just lucked out that morning at Centre-link. He met up with Harvey in the queue and being of a peaceful disposition offered up some advice about filling out the forms. That is when Harvey saw that Marvin's real name was Muhammad Khan. His racism came to the fore, his face screwed, and his mouth vented.

'You're a bloody bomb thrower Marvin!'

He continued for what seemed to Marvin an eternity, tormenting him about his name, his colour and Islam. Harvey was not bothered by the crowd, as he turned to walk away, now seemingly uninterested in getting his illegal government hand out, he scowled back in Marvin's direction.

'Stinking towel head!' Then he walked off.

Marvin had placed the disk of his life, in his top pocket. He felt overwhelmed by a lack of desired outcomes and warm conclusions. His plan was to cast it off the dam wall at the Lake. Somehow, he felt a ceremonious expression was needed to add closure to his current depressed state of mind. He knew that the only way ahead in life was to find peace. Like his faith and his Islamic culture, he was sure that eventually a balance could be found. His Pashtun tribal ancestry had given him the pillars of ancient morality that even predated his Islamic faith. They were Hospitality, Honour, Sanctuary and Retribution. He knew there was no honour in the hearts of some. He had found sanctuary and hospitality in the kindness of friends. Retribution, based on a Pashtun proverb 'a blow for a pinch', was not in his make-up, it was for souls who forgave little and lacked empathy. Marvin was above that.

The dam wall was a dangerous place at any time, but with dark clouds closing in on the last light of day, there was danger in every step. There was a twenty-metre drop to jagged rocks on the western side and a plunge into the deep brooding lake to the east. The dam wall was originally built in 1856 across Hunts Creek to provide drinking water for Parramatta's growing population. It has a single arch construction, one of only a dozen built since 100 BC, the first naturally by the Roman's. Built from Sydney sandstone blocks with a concrete capping, the surface was now covered with 150 years of grime, slime, and bird droppings. Marvin was being reckless, security spikes and barb wire placed at either end of the dam wall could not stop him on his mission.

He held on to the support rails and eased himself over the spikes. He now had a secure footing on the wall, but as he let go a piece of barbed wire gouged his hand and a trickle of blood splashed on to the still surface of the lake. Marvin wrapped a handkerchief around the cut and proceeded on all fours to the centre of the wall. He dangled his legs off the wall only inches off the glassy surface. It was strangely peaceful with the last light of day reflecting light in hypnotising eddies. He sat there with a slight smile of achievement on his face as his senses kicked in. The sweet call of a rosella caught his attention, as did the smell of duck droppings and musty lake water. A water rat the size of a small cat indignantly scurried off the other end of the dam wall when it saw Marvin's sunset silhouette. Apart from that, all was still.

He reached into his pocket and held the disk in his hand.

Annoyance with vacating tenants dumping rubbish on the council strip next to the bus stop and buses never running on time seemed like silly things to worry about. As was his fear of that idiot Harvey and his foolish bigotry. He smiled again when he thought of a dream, he had the night before last. In a lather of sweat he had come running down the stairs from his unit ready to chastise someone dumping a computer on the sidewalk, only to trip over a discarded picture of 'The Last Supper' and fall under the wheels of bus, that for once, was on time.

He raised his hand and with a parting prayer to his parents, cast the disk into the brooding depths. The water suddenly broiled with activity. Chilly water, a pain in his calf and a blow to his head were Marvin's final physical feelings. His mental extinction was a replay of happy childhood moments and of bright sunshine before his life force faded into the unknown.

CHAPTER 9

Bob Stickles

B ob Stickles was a good businessman with a genuine heart. Together with his mum Matilda, they ran the antique barn called 'Ma Stickles Emporium', just to the rear of the Rose and Thorn pub. These days the business limped on, fed by auctions, and deceased estates. Some said that a walk-through Ma Stickles barn was to take a walk through the history of Parramatta. Others called it an eyesore on progress and plotted its demise.

His great grandfather started the business in the mid 1800's when most of Parramatta streets were pot holed dirt tracks and creeks after summer storms. Back then, being only sixty years after the First Fleet arrived, antiques were rare. Most relics were called an antique after a twenty-year life, unless of course you managed to secure a Ship Captain's table or the like from some new colony gentry going bad. The main income earner in the old days, apart from locally made household items, was black market Rum. From these slightly illegal beginnings the Stickles family fortunes had its ups and downs, these days it just plodded along.

Bob sat still in a smelly old, cracked leather chair adjacent to an antique desk that was cluttered with invoices. He was concentrating and frowning at certain unpaid accounts. The business caused these moments more often lately, especially when he and his wife ventured on overseas trips. In Bobs mind they just soaked up profits with no material gain. The business was sound and kept viable by charming elderly widows and widowers ridding themselves of a lifetime worth of chattels and collectables that their recently departed loved ones had horded. These elderly shylocks were willing to part with most items, but never all their worldly goods and they always haggled over the price. This contrasted with the children of deceased estates. They were generally just keen to get rid of the junk so they could sell the old joint. Despite the profits, Bob was cynical about life's material needs and the owner's true worth.

At times, this cynicism boiled within him, and he just sat in his chair and stared at the well-worn surroundings of the Emporium. He saw the slight eddy currents of dust particles riding the waves of air movement, all made visible by the streams of light that made their way into the building via ancient holes and cracks within the structure. Bob had cracks in his own childhood structure to contend with, but they let truly little light in. His dad died of liver cancer in the late sixties. Being witness to his father's suffering had made Bob a non-drinker, a part time charity worker and an S.E.S volunteer.

He befriended a lot of the towns down and outs, that included Steve, Irish Mick, and Bruce the truckie. Occasionally he would buy them a meal at the Rose and Thorn, but never alcohol. When it came to a drink, Bob's beer was tea, either cold or hot depending on the season. As a kid he was bashed senseless on numerous occasions by a drunken father and was aware of alcohol's vicious ability to change certain characters for the worst. Apart from his sobriety talks, Bob was always handing out snippets of wisdom and just last week he was overheard dishing up some 'Forest Gump' gems to Bruce.

'Bruce!' he said, with a teacher's empathy. 'Remember that 'Life is like a box of chocolates', when you are young, they are all cold and hard to bite into, but as you age you heat them up with vitality. By the time you reach sixty they have all started to melt and as your memories start to fade all you are left with is a box of chocolate gloop. So, eat 'em up quick before they melt and don't worry about the tummy pains along the way, that's all part of living and dying.'

He was a funny and thoughtful mate to many. He always had a book in his hand and whenever he was cornered in discussion on the mystery of life or other deep subjects, his quotes were always amusing. He was not a religious man. But one quiet Sunday while talking with Steve and Mick at the barn, the topic of 'what's it all about?' came up. Bob was trying to explain their place in the scheme of things and was going on about the size of the Universe. In the end he just gave up, as no one was really on his wavelength and said, look,

'All we are is just a squeaky fart in a flatulent Universe!'

That got their attention and their laughter.

Bob's role in the State Emergency Service was that of Local Controller and he had recently encouraged Steve and Mick to become part time volunteers. He had talked them into joining as part of his 'way forward plan' in assuming a mentor role in their lives. It was a double-edged sword building self-esteem and controlling their drinking habits. Bob was also an optimist.

The weekend kicked off with a predicted steamy Saturday, which would be accompanied later by its mate, a late afternoon spring storm. Jake had arranged to meet Bob at Rosehill racecourse, prior to lunch with their wives in the Ascot room. They both enjoyed a little wager from time to time and it was a good opportunity to catch up with the local news and their mate Marvin's recent dilemma.

In 1883, work began on the Rosehill Horse Racing Track, on a portion of a land grant to John Macarthur. In 1885, the track was finished, and the first race meeting was held. Since those early days, the local punters have won and lost fortunes all in the name of reasoned chance. Then like now, colourful characters gave race day an air of villainy and shaded innuendo. High rollers and horse breeders from the upper land holding classes looked down from balconies and dining rooms at the riff-raff working classes, the bookies, and the bagmen with an air of accepted snobbery. But when the horses ran a commonality of wishful outcomes combined the whole gathering as one. Class differences were still there today but they were well hidden behind a veil of Australian 'tall poppy syndrome' and credit card wealth.

Men ruled the track for the first eighty years of horse racing development, but as time moved on, female jockeys, lady trainers and glamour took hold. Basically, because of female anti-discrimination lobbying, 'The Ladies Day' and the Melbourne Cup fashion carnivals became the norm. Today, women seem to outnumber the men. The

Parramatta area was renowned for grunge and easy wear fashions. So, on race day it is quite a spectacle to see a festoon of coloured dresses, large hats and sexy legs making their way across James Ruse Drive towards the track. All comers are bar and bet bound for a day of raunchy fun and showing off. The blokes are there also, their eyes darting and their wallets teasing to make some money on the horse flesh and impress the young ladies. The X and Y generations of men may not tuck their shirts in, but suits, hats and loose ties do show a general acceptance of race day class for a special social event.

The glue that underpins these days of horses, money and fine fillies is alcohol, so the bar takings would be on a par with the TAB and bookie takings. Like most things in life, when there is money and grog involved, crime is not taking the day off. The racetrack was always a magnet to life worn characters. They bent and often broke the law with varying degrees of success. In the past they were tagged as 'Colourful Sydney Racing Identities'. They were either thugs or nobles of unscrupulous intent and in some cases both. The laundering of tainted money was their game and horse racing added colour and excitement as the detergent to successful wealth creation. Today's batch of clever crooks had other ways of washing their dirty money, within legitimate businesses. They were more like 'Rainbow Larrikins' than colourful identities. They were the human equivalent to a Rainbow Lorikeet, vibrant, aggressive, and greedy in dividing up the spoils of life's handouts.

One such character who frequented the Rosehill track was Rikos Hassan. Friends and acquaintances knew him affectionately or nervously as Rick. He was born in the early seventies in Beirut and came to Australia as a refugee. His family were dirt poor and not shy at acquiring what they needed by any means available. In this environment Rick was a great student, Australia was a pot of gold compared to what they had left behind. An orb spider's web on a bush track summed up Rick's present world. His lattice of criminal connections around town would twitch to any movement of appeal. If it were away from him, he would get vicious and pounce. If it approached him, he would take it in and wrap it up in a bundle of silk for future devouring. Harvey Maitland was one of Rick's latest bundles.

In the last ten years Rick had blossomed from a nasty misogynous petty criminal and pimp to an entrepreneur. He was a knight of the realm in Western Sydney's seedy, but lucrative business of night clubs, slave prostitution and cocaine imports. To those on the right side of the law he ran a successful Import/Export company called 'Rikos Developments Pty Ltd'. His ego placed him on a higher plane than his associates, but the conversation always fell back to his material wealth. Whether it was his flash new Lamborghini with the Russian Chauffeur Dmitry or a four-million-dollar beach house purchase, he wanted people to know he was successful. With his solarium tan and his long black gelled ponytail, unknown to him, most people had a first impression that he looked like a Columbian drug lord. What was true was that this poor Lebanese kid from the back streets of Auburn had done well for himself.

Jake had no knowledge of Rick, but he did know the character who he was talking to near the bookies stand, it was the weird looking pirate that walked past him down at the lake. Harvey had a reputation around town as a no hoper, flawed from birth and bred to be a loser, but

Jake was not aware that this low life was the bloke that had recently given Marvin a tough time. The twitchy lake walker looked well out of place talking to a character with polished assets. A Gucci leather coat and Italian leather shoes on the Steven Segal look-a-like contrasted with the street urchins grunge pirate look. They seemed a strange match to be in a heavy conversation. The thought faded as Jake saw Bob standing near the door to the Ascot room.

'Hi Bob, ready for some winnings?'

'Sounds alright to me Jake, any useful tips?'

'Yeah, just one, 'Ankle Deep' is running in the first and after a week of rain, a soft track and a light weight on his back it's got to be worth fifty bucks on a place ticket.'

'Where's your balls Jake, with that prescience form guide in your head it should be worth one hundred on the nose.'

'One hundred is the days budget Bob and that includes lunch. Unlike you, I like a couple of full-strength beers at weeks end, the bars that way!'

'Ok iced tea and VB coming right up, you place the bets!'

'By the way how's Marvin going Bob?'

Bob had always been a 'Good Samaritan' and when he had found out about the ordeal Marvin went through prior to coming to Parramatta he managed to help him find some part-time work.

'No one has seen him since last week Jake! Steve said he rang Marvin about a mowing job on Tuesday and left a message. He also told me about his depressed state. I hope he hasn't done anything stupid mate.'

'He's no fool Bob, just suffering from a bit of anxiety. He may have just gone to see that cousin of his in Melbourne.'

'I know, I thought that myself at first, but Jake, he tells me everything and after that bit about casting away his demons on a disk, I'm real worried. I rang the cops yesterday and reported him as a missing person. I had to go down to Phillip St and fill out a report.'

'That may have been a bit premature Bob!'

'I don't care Jake they said they will check into it, in the meantime the boys from the pub are keeping a look out for him.'

'Well, I'm going for a walk down the lake in the morning, I will ask Bill and Fritz if they have seen him.'

'By the way Jake, see that bloke over there with the red braces that's Harvey, the moron who gave Marvin a tough time.'

'Hey Bob, I saw him down at the lake last week, he had a real mean look in his eyes. He was also just talking to a real up-town Steven Segal type down at the bookies stand. You might mention that little get together and Marvin's run in with Harvey to the cops as well.'

'Good point Jake, I'll tell 'em about that on Monday.'

'Come on Bob, he'll turn up, don't let that wreck our luck today. Let's just have some fun and worry tomorrow, the girls will be here soon!'

'Ok mate, you're probably right, how about 'Anxious Gal' in the third at Flemington?'

'Now you're talking mate, so get those drinks!'

The day progressed with mixed successes, laughter, and a smattering of bullshit or as Jake called it extrapolated truths. Bob was sipping his cold tea and Jake was starting to feel empathy with the world in general. That is the way it is with social sessions and alcohol, some people should never touch the stuff, whereas others go silent, silly, or sad. By the time the ladies arrived Jake was in a great mood, somewhere between silent and silly. Anne picked up on it straight away and ordered a lemon lime and bitters with the meal.

'Looks like I'll be driving home, eh Jake?'

'Thanks babe, you're my love taxi.'

'That's ok Jake, you can drive home next weekend after the re-union.'

'And that's fair enough.' Smirked Jake, knowing full-well they would be catching a cab both ways to the year's big event.

Helen Stickles sat opposite Jake, he could tell immediately she wanted to tell him all about her recent trip to Europe to visit her mum. But Jake dragged it out a bit longer by asking whether Bob and she were going to attend the re-union.

'We wouldn't miss it Jake, as a matter of fact I have organised a bit of a surprise for the class of sixty-nine.'

'Ok out with it!'

'No way Jake you will just have to wait and see!'

That snookered Jake to get back to the European vacation. As he sat there listening to the highlights of Paris, with its romantic icons and Tuscany with its quaint villages, vineyards, and walks. Jake felt that glow of envy that comes from other people's overseas trips. He knew that for the next week Anne would be making plans for their next offshore adventure.

Helen was a lady of grace, she told her story with gesture

and passion in her eyes,

'Well at least the left one', thought Jake. Helen's right eye was made of glass, the sad result of a misfired skyrocket on a bonfire night back in the sixties. The eye did not always follow the conversation around the table.

The day came to an end too soon, the crowd was getting noisier and the attractive mini-skirted race-day ladies where wobbling at the knees.

'I think it's time we headed for home Jake.'

'Ok by me Anne, I have broken even with the bets and the food, and we are only over budget by five bucks. Catch up next weekend Bob, by the way who's watching the shop?'

'My star recruits, Irish Mick and Steve are Jake, and I hope they turned in a profit today to make up for my poor form and their stupidity!'

'What did they do now Bob?'

'They left the shutter half up last night; lucky I walked that way home just after closing time eh! I'll be having words with the pair of 'em on Monday.'

In a soup of blurred thoughts and strange shadows, Steve heard Bob talking. The words 'bugger them useless bastards,' filtered in his subconscious and filled him with fresh pain. A shutter door slammed shut, a car started, and a tom cat wailed all in unison to his throbbing head. As the musky smell of old alcohol aroused his senses, a filtered ray of daylight through a barred window struck him like a sledgehammer. One eye scanned the surroundings and slowly began to focus.

In the corner lay his good mate Mick. All arms and legs, spread-eagled amongst broken bottles, shelves and a busted phone. His memory started to flood back, at least as far as the fight. Like a lightning bolt in a storm, Steve suddenly flinched,

'Oh no Mick, it's Saturday'.

'Yeah, so what'!

'The shutters locked! Bob's going to the Racecourse!'

'You mean we're stuck in this antique shit hole till Monday morning?'

'Brilliant! I've got lawns to mow.'

'What will we do, we'll starve?'

'Now don't go into a panic Mick, let's just rest a while and think of a way out of here.'

'Where is the phone?'

'Broken, ripped off the wall!'

'Try screaming for help.'

'Always optimistic aren't you Mick, who will hear us out here in the barn?'

'Don't forget that you're the reason we're stuck here in the first place, with your smart mouthing about being reliable!'

'Now don't start that argument again Mick, just drop it.'

'Steve, how come Bob didn't find us when he came back from the city last night?'

'What makes you think he came back?'

'Somebody locked the shutter, ya' keg head!'

'He probably didn't see us in the dark and just locked up. Hey Mick, I suppose he thinks were still just a couple of unreliable drunks!'

'Well, I'll be putting him straight Steve, I couldn't take another of that sobriety prevents liver cancer speeches of his.'

'You know what really makes me angry Mick?'

'What?'

'Those shop-lifters, gave us a caning over a couple of pieces of junk.'

'We don't know if it was junk Steve, it may have been worth something to Bob. They seem to know what they wanted and where it was. You know what really makes me angry mate?'

'What?'

'That school re-union is on down at the Lake next Saturday, and apart from the old farts from Arthur Phillip High, some of the eye candy from Anne's office might be going.'

'So, what's the issue?'

'Well, we will look like a pair of bruised and battered losers.'

'Great! Like I said, you are always the optimist.

CHAPTER 10

Harry Moffitt

D etective sergeant Harry Moffitt was a good cop. He had done the hard yards from traffic to drugs. Through it all, the corruption, and the changes at the top he had kept his head above water. At times he had unwillingly bent with all the other trees in the forest of law enforcement and political interference. He was a survivor.

Harry now believed that in general there were three prime directives in life. From birth to twelve it was fun. Then to age sixty it was basically money and sex. From sixty it is down-hill till death where the prime directive is money and health. You only have to listen to conversation amongst these groups to reinforce this premise. With this thought in mind, he realised that he only had about six years left to make the most of it before his bodily decline became the main talking point. His first wife Lucy died several years back after suffering from breast cancer. Despite radical surgery, chemo, radiation treatment and new wonder drugs Lucy lost the fight, and he lost his love. His agnostic view of life and his cynicism were reinforced by her death on their wedding anniversary. This period of his life affected him greatly. He withdrew into his work and for two years remained hardened and alone. That was until he met Molly. She was what most men his age needed. Vivacious, active and ten years younger, her personality and attitude brought Moffitt back to the land of the living. The bonus was sex and company.

These days he was more secure, and his experiences carried him on waves of confidence and caution. The young constables liked working with him. He had a gift of passing on the important stuff without the bullshit. The academy gave the new cops effective communication skills and the principles of basic law, but true policing skills could only be found at the coal face. Harry knew that the limits had fuzzy edges and that information at times was more important than arrests.

Rather than bust a young tagger for graffiti or affray, a young offender would get Harry's boot up the bum and taken for a drive out of town that led to a considerable walk home. Courts were not always the solution. The process of charging, paperwork, and court appearances often found the offender back on the streets with a warning and paint can in hand the following night. Humans give respect for the strangest reasons and sometimes Harry reaped rewards and information on those higher up the criminal food chain, from these same taggers.

Harry had friends and enemies in Parramatta and lots of acquaintances, but they all knew him as just plain Moffitt. He was an early riser who loved the dawn of a new day and the pre-peopled peace. Afternoon shifts were his favourite, morning walks always started at his driveway in

Sullivan Road. He would do a slow jog down to the start
of Brickfield Street then walk to the river, onto the ferry
wharf and head home via Parramatta Park, the Leagues
Club, and the back streets of North Parramatta.

To Moffitt, Brickfield Street was the international date
line of Parramatta, a smorgasbord of nations. To walk
with him was to walk with a focussed beam of thought.
The trivial things did not pass him by. Coupled with his
knowledge on the history of the area, he was aware of his
surroundings and could sense its mood and mischief. His
mind was always on the job, absorbing details like water
to a sponge. He would smile at the bizarre and frown
with a cold stare at malice.

He knew Mrs Baker at the top end of Brickfield Street
would be out hosing her hydrangeas and give him a cursory wave as he passed. He knew of her current run in
with the Korean neighbours over their children's Saturday piano lessons and her complaints of constant noise.
He also knew that her husband who recently died had
suffered in Burma during the war and he knew how she
referred to all Asians as 'those Jap's'. Conflict settlement
was so much easier when a cop was armed with such
knowledge.

Further on down Brickfield, where the fifty's fibro
houses made way to modern villas and units that were
festooned by junk mail and shopping trolleys, the cultures met. This was where the cooking smells of different
nations and the background chatter of many languages
held stories of struggle and sacrifices just to get a foot
hold. He knew some of the characters on the wrong side
of the law that lived there also, the dealers, the taggers,
the wife beaters, and some of the local gang members. He

also knew that the bad eggs were only a small percentage of the good. That the basket was also overflowing with goodwill, charity and hard workers all bent on giving their children a solid foundation in life.

He knew Aussie Alf on the corner of Grose Street, who decked his house out with EEL's memorabilia and always had a comment on the politics of rugby league. He knew Imad, his wife Heber from Iran and their beautiful daughters who with gentle Mandaen faith always offered a treat or a smile when passing. Further on down Brickfield Street, across the busy Victoria Road and on to Elizabeth Street stood the iconic All Saints Church where many of the locals had been married. He knew its meeting hall and its echoes of past dances. His next steps found him approaching the river and the exploding food smells of India. He knew the Kumars and the Singhs and their strong sons with great cricket potential. He recollected the joke he played on Harrandath Kumar when he issued a ticket for parking his wheelie bin in a pre-pay spot. He knew to avoid the days when the bins of all nations curdled the street air with the refuse of left-over culinary creations and to avoid the quarterly rubbish pick up days that cluttered the paths with enough used material to furnish Mogadishu.

Moffitt walked on over the Rowers Bridge. As he passed Falals Lebanese restaurant he recalled last year's Christmas party, a feast of great food and the voluptuous belly dancer, who had him up on the floor swivelling his hips to haunting Arabian music. Momentarily he thought of the global economic troubles and feared that some of these fine eateries would shortly close and that the Centre link unemployment queues would lengthen, and crime would grow.

Across Phillip Street and up to George Street, Moffitt walked on, passing Vinnie's and the Salvos realising that flamboyant recessioniters would soon be searching the clothing racks to keep pace with style and changes throughout the challenging times ahead. When he got to the crossroads of Church and George streets, he looked east, back to the Roxy theatre. He remembered that as a boy, it was the 'Taj Mahal' of Parramatta, 'the place to go' on a Saturday night. To yesterday's youth, it was 'Hop-along Cassidy' matinees or a 'John Wayne' cowboy movie. Today, it was the favourite watering hole of the 'me-too' generation with short skirts, pills, muscles, and fights. To some, the frequent fights between rival Skip and Lebanese gangs gave it an atmosphere of fear, but cops like Moffitt, knew better. He understood the currents of crime, the corruption and stand over tactics they gave such places their vibrant appeal.

Looking north from the crossroads, through a cops eyes, he imagined the overweight European gents in tacky suits sitting at their favourite coffee spot at 'Eat' street. That is where they would sit smoking cigars and whispering business or underworld rumours, their gold teeth reflecting in the morning light, while their sweaty moustaches swam in the coffee cream. From the same vantage point looking south past the old Saint John's church, its courtyard and mall, he visualised the street wanderers, unshaven, unkempt, and unwanted. Their nights were spent sleeping on park benches in a somewhat uncaring city, with their presence only discernible by their odour.

Moffitt left the thought behind and headed west toward Parramatta Park and through the Tudor Gates on O'Connell Street. These gates were built in 1885 marking an entry point that was established in 1788. Two years later

Arthur Phillip built a one-bedroom cottage that would evolve over the following years to Government House and the possibility of Parramatta becoming the seat of power in a new land. Before Moffitt was a window of history that stood now as an icon to what might have been. He paused to tie his shoelace and noticed the Oak tree monument and headstone to Lady Mary Fitzroy that marked the day and place she died, 7th December 1847. For a moment he pondered the way a single event can shape history.

In that thought a reflection back in time could have found Lady Mary staring at her image in a decorative pewter table mirror. On the bed was a partially finished patchwork quilt, it was to be a colourful reminder of her other far away home and her grandmother's flower garden. She was powdering her fine features in preparation for a day's outing with her husband, Sir Charles Fitzroy, Governor of the Colony. Sir Charles loved her deeply and loved the thought of making Parramatta his seat of power, in a traditional English capital. It would be pleasantly positioned, upstream from its port where fresh water met the salt water.

Sir Charles called out that the carriage was ready. For a moment Mary paused and looked out the window to the sparkling river crescent. In the distance she could see crops growing in the fertile soil and cows entering the dairy for their daily milking. She sighed at the beauty in her life. This diverse land offered challenges, but deep within she knew this home could be her castle, this river her Thames and this growing town her London. She walked down the stairs and out the door to a bright summer morning and the smile of her husband who assisted her into the carriage. The Aid-de-camp Lieutenant

Masters beckoned the horses on, they bolted and minutes later Lady Mary lay dead at the foot of one Oak tree in a corridor of Oaks that led down George Street to the river port. Lieutenant Masters died later. Sir Charles was heartbroken and seldom returned to Parramatta. His dreams were shattered and, in that moment, so were Parramatta's, it seemed destined to always be 'Sydney's working-class Cinderella'.

Moffitt walked on and just for a moment had a strange anxious feeling of lost opportunity. The feeling passed quickly. He continued his journey through the park to the Riverside Café and stopped for his usual morning coffee. The new lessee was a friend, Lilly Lue Tang and she had big plans for the Café. This included a name change to 'Lilly's Tea House' and a development plan along the lines of the Chinese Gardens in Sydney. Her idea would capture a growing need in the Parramatta area for multi-cultural venues. Moffitt stood there for a moment and took in the splendid river view that was filtered by jacaranda trees, now in full bloom. It was a beautiful part of the city. The adjacent building made it even more special, it was the 'Governors Dairy' one of the oldest buildings in Australia. Built by George Salter around 1798 it is a rare surviving work-a-day cottage and it had recently won a world heritage listing.

Another friend of Moffitt, a New Zealander and entrepreneur from Christchurch, was seeking a licence to run a Punt boat ride, like the Venice equivalent, from the Bernie Banton Bridge to Little Coogee at the rear of the Leagues club. Moffitt had witnessed momentous changes in Parramatta through his life and he could only see a bright future ahead. Cinderella may be still in the kitchen, but one day we would get our glass slipper.

As he walked in the door at home his phone rang! It was his new offsider, Joan Debono. She was fresh from the city and as keen as mustard. All her early days as a uniform were spent in the Lakemba region. She had a good bit of experience with Mid-Eastern crime gangs, so Moffitt was happy to help her with her rise through the detective ranks. She also was tall and big boned, with a build like an Amazon warrior. This could come in handy if Moffitt needed back up.

The other good thing about having a female on the team was information gathering. The 'good cop, bad cop' routine always worked better when the good cop had a pretty face.

'We have a problem Bones?' It was funny how nicknames suited certain people.

'Yeah boss, Bob Stickles from the barn reported his Afghan mate Marvin Khan, hasn't been seen for a while and some of the blokes at the Rose and Thorn reckon he may have topped himself down at the lake.'

'Ok mate I'll pick you up at the station in a half an hour.'

Detective Moffitt's eyebrows rose at the sight of the approaching park caretaker. Fritz was armed with a garden blower in each hand and dressed to amuse. A bright yellow reflecting vest, an upsized pair of king-gee shorts tied at the waste with a cord, blue rubber washing gloves, leather calf spats, blunder-stone boots and to top it off a wide brim blue hat for sun protection. He stood there like a vandalised statue. Peppered gold and grey stubble on his chiselled jaw was highlighted by these bright blue eyes that were penetrating the detectives mind as he approached. Fritz had a notable limp.

'Fritz, is it? I'm Senior Detective Moffitt and this is Detective Debono, your sister Mary at the Café said you may be able to help us with our investigation into the disappearance of a local lad.'

'Yeah, what's his name?'

'Marvin Khan!'

'Yeah, heard the name, what's the story?'

'A few of his friends at the Rose & Thorn pub are concerned about his welfare and have informed us that he has been missing for a week or more. They mentioned that he may have been depressed and was going on about visiting the lake. Have you seen any unusual activity down here recently?'

'No not unless you call those moronic graffiti artists unusual! The bastards went the rats with their spray cans on some of the overhang caves on the lake walk, sometime in the last week. One idiot does not even scribble, he prints the name 'JOHN', I do not know whether its toilet humour or his trying to be different. Either way it's vandalism, so why won't you blokes ban or fine the mugs who sell the paint? That's the answer!'

'You may be right Fritz, take it up with your local member but we're here on this other matter.'

'Yeah, well that's the only odd thing I can think of detective. Wait a minute, I did pick up a strange bit of rubbish the other day down near the dam wall, a pyjama top. Thought to myself maybe a sleep-walker must've taken a fall!'

'Who's that?'

'It had some blood on the sleeve! On second thoughts it probably belonged to one of those nuts from Cumberland Mental Hospital. They are always walking on that side of the lake on their way to Billy Chan's butcher shop for the free Wednesday sausage sizzle. People always want something for nothing these days'.

'Do you still have it?'

'No, pegged it out with the rest of this week's garbage.'

'Pity, but thanks for your help anyhow Fritz. By the way how did you get that limp?'

'Oh, it's nothing, skinned it on a rock picking up the floating rubbish that those weekend towel heads leave lying around. But I suppose if it were not for them and the Chinese, I wouldn't have this great job. Most of the 'real Aussies' head for the beach on weekends, don't they?'

'Not very politically correct are you Fritz? By the way aren't you, German?'

'No but my father was!'

'War service for Hitler, I'll bet.'

'Only regular army, he made sergeant.'

'Well, there's been a lot of water under the bridge since then Fritz, it's time to move on and accept people on merit.'

'I will when I see some merit detective, but I won't hold my breath.'

'All the same, could you keep an eye out around here and let us know if you see anything out of the ordinary, we will be in contact.'

Moffitt walked off with the look of annoyance on his face, leaving Joan to give Fritz contact details, along with her good cop face. This had proved itself on numerous occasions as a means of getting extra information from witnesses, especially arrogant ones.

As Moffitt walked back towards the car, he scanned the dam wall and reed area near the bridge. Wood ducks were trailing across the water and guinea fowl were squawking. They had all just helped themselves to a feast of bread, compliments of some kids and their parents. Someone had even thrown a grapefruit or orange into the mix. He began to think that Fritz may be right about the rubbish problem down here.

Bones got back to the car just as a call came in for a knife attack in Westfield's shopping centre.

'Looks like this investigation may have to wait a while Bones, how did you go with Fritz?'

'He may have some issues, but he seems to really care about this place. From what I gathered he does not miss much. I'm sure he will give us a call, even if it's just to have a whinge.'

The next day Moffitt's first port of call was Stickles Emporium. He caught Bob feet up in his old leather chair and snoozing in the morning sun with a book on his lap.

'It's ok for some Bob.'

'Just resting my eyelids thanks Moffitt.'

'Any word yet on your mate Marvin?'

'No mate, not a peep, I'm really starting to get worried for the young bloke, he has had a hard trot in life and it's about time he got a better deal.'

'Don't fret too much Bob we're on the case.'

'Feel like a cuppa tea Moffitt?'

'I wouldn't say no mate, I need something to wash the

cobwebs out.'

Bob went on with a bit of Marvin's history while making the tea.

'Ok then Bob, now tell me more about this dust up between your mate Marvin and this Maitland character?'

'You've got that wrong mate. Marvin would not hurt a fly and could not fight his way out of a wet paper-bag. This low life Harvey only gave Marvin a verbal bashing at Centre-link because he saw that he was a Muslim. But I do know something that might be of interest, Jake McCooey said he saw Harvey walking around the lake during the week, like he owned the place. He also saw him talking to some hi-roller dude with a ponytail at the racetrack on Saturday.'

'Look Bob I know this bloke Maitland; I've watched his career from his teens to the gutter and I think the ponytail guy might be an up-town crook from Sydney called Rick. What I can't work out is common ground between the two.'

'Well, Jake said they looked pretty chummy.'

'Maybe Rick is recruiting some fresh staff in Parra? Anyhow thanks for the tips. I will place them in my top draw, but I will not jump to any quick conclusions Bob, let's just hope your mate turns up in the next day or two. Thanks for the cuppa, I best be off.'

CHAPTER 11

Pham Quang and Pham Ly

It was in May of the year 1975 that Pham Quang and his new bride Ly made their escape. Saigon was in turmoil; the Americans had fled and people like the Phams had to make their own plans. Their choices were scarce. If they stayed the new Communist masters from Hanoi would either have them executed or placed in a re-education camp. Most of their extended family had been killed in a bold wave of Vietcong forces that had swamped Saigon over the past months. Their situation was desperate, and then fate or luck stepped in with a chance of survival. Pham Quang was a clerk in one of South Vietnams civil service departments, his section manager and friend had secured a place on a boat for both Quang and his wife. The escape would put them both in great danger, but they had to try. Other fleeing people were being shot at random in the fear and excitement of victory and defeat, but there was still hope.

It was in the early hours of the morning on a rain-mist beach south of the now newly named Ho Chi Minh City that fifty people, on a boat made for ten, bid farewell to their homeland. The voyage was a nightmare of rough seas and little food. Three souls were lost overboard, and a mother died in childbirth within the first few days heading south. Their situation seemed hopeless. As the food and water ran out, the passengers sat and laid in the sad silence of pending death. Then, three weeks into the journey they awoke on a bright still day to see the shape of an Australian naval frigate on the horizon, a fortuitous encounter that led to their survival.

From Darwin to the Villawood detention centre in Western Sydney the Pham family had smiles on their faces. Eventually a home, albeit a small flat, was found for them in the village of Cabramatta. Many refugees from Vietnam in those chaotic times joined them in the same area. It would take thirty years and a lot of teething issues around drugs and crime but all these strangers in a strange land would succeed in making Cabramatta the vibrant town it is today.

The Pham family went on to improve their lives and gather wealth. Both were loners and other than attending church on Sundays, they kept to themselves. Quang secured a part-time clerical job and Ly found a sewing job in a local factory. Their earnings were low at first, but their savings grew. Disappointment came their way with news that Ly would never have children, but their love was strong. Within their history of struggle, they both knew that happiness was found in their own company. As time went on, they invested in property and planned for a holiday. They purchased two properties over the following years. One was in Cabramatta, which would be their home and another in North Parramatta that would be their retirement income.

The Sorrell Street property in North Parramatta was a bargain. It was from a deceased estate and had been vacant for some time. The estate agent had shown them through on a couple of occasions and it was obvious a lot of work would be required. There were also signs that vagrants had been living rough on site. This did not put the Pham's off the purchase, they were both hard workers. It would take months to ready the place for rental and following that they had planned a trip back to a now stable Vietnam. It would be a sad and happy occasion. Their homeland had improved greatly and now that they were Australian citizens any fear of arrest had gone. They had been in contact recently with some cousins from their old village and a family re-union party had been arranged. Both Quang and Ly felt blessed with what life had provided. They loved Australia for the fresh start it had given them and now in their twilight years they could relax a little.

On the day of the Pham family first house inspection, Pat Maitland was having a sleep in. He heard a car in the driveway, quickly gathered his swag and went out the broken back door. He was cornered in the back yard, so he crawled under the house and waited. Quang and Ly were excited with the house and told the real estate agent of all their plans in relation to their pending retirement and overseas holiday. Pat laid there in silence and listened to the whole story. Opportunity had knocked. He was starting to feel the pain of a hard life and had tired of the constant moving. Old age was finally catching up and a more permanent address was needed. For the last few months, he had camped out at night in this run-down shack. After spending most of his life as a man of no fixed address change was now in the wind.

A month later the Vietnamese couple finally purchased the place and were busy giving it a spruce up for rent. Pat had to move back to some of his rough sleeping haunts in Parramatta to make his plans but kept a daily eye on the Pham's progress.

A chilly wind from the south and intermittent squalls of rain ruled out his usual open-air camp. On a clear evening, the street people of Parramatta have some favourite locations. One is the rotunda in Parramatta Park opposite Lilly's Tea House. It is out of the way and has a low brick wall for protection. Another is a park bench in front of the old Kings School site. On extremely cold nights however, Pat knew the Rigby Parking station stair well would be the warmest. Pat was not first to arrive, two shopping trolleys full of second-hand possessions blocked the door. He pushed them aside and entered to find the best spots already occupied by old Jock and the Weed, as he was affectionately known. They were well into a flagon of wine and offered Pat a swig. He grabbed the flagon and told the pair to piss off out of his spot. A fight broke out, but Jock and the Weed were no match for an aggressive Pat. They succumbed to his knife wielding threats and moved on to another haunt. Pat would spend the night alone again and that is the way he preferred it. While laid out on the cold floor of the stair well, drinking the last of the free flagon, he finalised his plan for a more permanent abode and the Sorrell Street property was perfect.

He awoke the next morning feeling miserable. His head was throbbing with the aftereffects of the flagon of wine. Slowly he made his way to the Parramatta Care soup kitchen in Villiers Street. It was to be a special treat day. A real three course meal was being served for a change. It was more for the benefit of some visiting politicians who wished to show the street people how much they cared. As Pat reached the head of the queue, he realised the Premier himself had his sleeves rolled up and was dishing out the mash. Cynicism peaked in Pat because he knew it was all about a photo opportunity for the voting public. He was not in any way moved by the experience, if anything his thoughts were to spit in the face of this heavy fat-faced, smiling suit. The joke was that he was not going to even vote at the coming elections, but a free meal was a free meal.

Over the following weeks Pat monitored the progress of restoration work that Pham Quang and Ly had undertaken. Now was the time to put his plan into action. It took some persuasion, but he managed to get a small loan from his sister-in-law Jill. He gave her the hard luck story about his need to find a more permanent place to live. He went on about his pain and how old age had finally caught up. Her heart felt for him, she was a fragile woman with deep empathy for sad cases and she knew he had had a difficult life. Pat secured enough money to pay the Phams a bond and one month's rent in advance. The only catch was that Harvey had to move in also and 'he could help with the rent,' Jill said. Pat had no intention of using the bond money for a lease agreement. It was only to show Quang and Ly his good intention and that he had the means to be a good tenant.

After a month of surveillance, Pat had established a pattern to the Pham's comings and goings. He had also overheard most of their travel plans and knew that they were now desperate to find the right tenant. Most importantly, he had heard them speaking of avoiding the cost of a real estate agent's fee for the lease and maintenance. It was after all, a sizable percentage of their rent money. Two weeks before Quang and Ly were due to fly out to Vietnam, Pat prepared himself. He used some of the money Jill had given him to purchase some clean clothes. Not new of course. Pat would never waste money on such trivial things, alcohol was far more important. The local Saint Vincent de Paul shop provided just what he was looking for. This included a sports jacket and matching pants. He wanted that professional business look. He folded the garments up in plastic to keep the fresh and ironed appearance and placed them in his swag.

The last night before he put his scam into action was pleasantly mild, so he spent it on the park bench opposite the Old Kings School site. The bulk of Jill's money was in a newly purchased second-hand wallet. His idea was to impress the Phams that he had the ability to pay his way. Not wishing people in Parramatta to see him suddenly change, he made his way by train to the men's shelter in Sydney. He then, for the first time in three months, had a shower and a general clean up. On the same day he also had a haircut and shave. On his return trip to Parramatta, he saw his reflection in a shop window and was a little shocked. In his entire life he thought that he had never looked so good. As far as he was concerned, he could now pass for any of the businesspeople who would normally ignore him on 'Sleep Street'.

His plan involved setting up a chance encounter, while he was supposedly walking to work. He waited by some trees close to the Pham's new house. An old Hyundai sedan pulled up in the driveway and as they stepped from the car Pat made his move.

'Good morning, lovely day.' Pat was smiling, while casually walking by.

Quang and Ly normally were shy of strangers, but this well-dressed businessman with a happy smile caught their attention.

'Yes, it is!' replied Quang. 'I hope it stays this way and you have a good day.'

This was just the opening Pat needed.

'Yes, I will thank you, I noticed the house was sold.' He continued. 'Do you know if the new owners are going to lease it?'

Quang and Ly looked at each other, feigning excitement, with their eyes acknowledging an opportunity.

'As a matter of fact, we are the owners and yes we are looking for a tenant. Are you interested?'

'Well yes, that is if the rent is in my budget range?' Pat was starting to enjoy the scam.

'I just moved my business to Parramatta and this house is an ideal location. Not only that but I have been living with my brother and his family, not that I don't love the kids, but they can be a challenge.'

Quang was impressed, a businessman with family in the area, and obviously just the type of tenant they had been looking for.

'Well, if you have the time, we could discuss it now.'

'Yes, I am a touch early for an appointment, I suppose I could have a look through the place.'

Pat shook hands with the pair. Then after introductions followed them into the house, commenting as he went on the smell of fresh paint and new fixtures.

'This is just what I have been looking for, what Real Estate agents are you using?'

'You look like a trustworthy gentleman. We thought we might avoid the unnecessary expense of agents and just have a signed lease agreement between us. Would that be ok with you?'

'Well normally I would prefer the legal way of conducting a leasing agreement, but you look like honest people. How much rent do would you want Quang?'

'We were thinking in the range of $600 a week, but because there will be no agent commission how does $550 sound Pat?'

'$500 would sound better,' smirked Pat, now feeling worthy of an 'Academy Award'.

'Then it's a deal!' said Quang. While smiling at his wife, nodding his head, and frantically shaking Pat's hand.

'I will get a lease agreement drawn up this week. There is only one problem, we are flying out to Vietnam next Thursday and we were hoping to have this all sorted out by then.'

'That's ok,' said Pat, opening his wallet full of cash. 'How about I give you four weeks rent in advance and how does a thousand sound for a bond?'

'That's fine,' said Quang, but keep your money for now, we will fix it up next week if that's ok.'

'Well, take at least a hundred.' Pat responded, while handing over the cash. 'I will feel secure in the deal then.'

'Thank you, Pat, how does next Tuesday sound, that will give Ly and I some time to finish off a few things around here.'

'Tuesday and Wednesday are out sorry Quang I have a conference in town.'

'Then it will have to be Thursday, we have a 3.00pm flight, would early morning be, ok?'

'That's ok with me Quang, I will move my stuff in on the following weekend and we will catch up with the bank deposit details when you return. I truly hope you have an enjoyable holiday.'

Pat was starting to think he had missed out on his true calling in life. 'I'm a professional bull-shit artist.' He thought to himself.

'Thanks Pat, yes we are really looking forward to it.'

'Ok Quang and Ly, I will see you both next weeks, I best be off now, thanks again.'

As Pat walked off, the Phams cuddled each other, they were so happy. Pat was happy too, but for a more sinister reason. These Vietnamese suckers played straight into his hands. It was 9.00 am and the bottle shop would be open in an hour, a drink was long overdue.

The following Wednesday night Pat broke in through the new back door of the Pham's house.

'I may as well spend a comfortable night in my new home,' he thought to himself.

However, it was a restless night's sleep. He was calculating all the things that could go wrong with his plan. It had nothing to do with guilt over his murderous intent, it was just the planning of it. Finally, the body and car disposal thoughts were washed away with a bottle of whiskey, and he dosed off. The next morning, he got up early and looked around the house at the Pham's wonderful renovation work. In a toolbox by the window, he found a lump hammer, it was just what he needed. He placed it on the kitchen sink, and suddenly felt the thrill of life. That expectation feeling was a leftover from his childhood days, which sadly always went unfulfilled.

It was a fine day with a soft breeze blowing from the south. Someone nearby was cooking sausages and the smell gave Pat a hungry feeling, but that could wait a while. After a wash he put on his business clothes. He secured his sheaf knife in its shin strap and waited out by the trees for the Phams to arrive. His suit was now a bit crumpled, and he had whiskey on his breath, but he was not concerned at his unshaven appearance. The Phams would only have the pending holiday and their flight time on their minds. Once he had the signed lease agreement none of that mattered anyhow.

As the car pulled up, Pat walked up smiling. The happy couple hopped out and their smiles faded slightly at Pat's unkempt condition. Pat picked up on the body language.

'Good morning Quang and Ly, sorry about the way I look. The conference ended up being an all-night affair, I only just made it back in time.'

'That's ok Pat, I hope it was a success?'

'Yes, I made some lucrative connections if you know what I mean.' Pat was back to playing the part.

'We are so pleased for you.' Quang replied. 'It's a wonderful day, isn't it? We are so looking forward to our trip.'

'Yes, you should enjoy Vietnam at this time of year, did you bring the lease?'

Pat's patience with the banter was now waning a little. He looked around and was pleased to note that there were no nosey people in the area.

'Yes, all signed and awaiting your approval, shall we go inside?'

'Yes, let's get this over with, so you pair can be on your way.'

The word 'signed' was just what he wanted to hear; the place was now legally his if anyone asked. Not that anyone he could think of would, especially if the Phams decided they liked Vietnam so much that they extended their stay.

'Yes', he thought to himself, I could be living here well into old age.

Behind Pat's smiling veneer his evil intention grew like hunger pains. Killing this happy couple was of no more concern to him than the time he worked in the Abattoir at Homebush, when he was younger. The hapless cows and the Phams were, after all, just red meat.

Pat followed the Pham's into the house. Ly was in front of him, she would be the first victim. He closed the door as he entered and pulled out his sheaf knife. As Quang walked past the kitchen bench, he noticed the lump hammer. He could not remember leaving it out. That is when he noticed the back door had been forced in. Pat grabbed the hammer and let fly across the scull of an unsuspecting Ly. She went down in a crumpled heap and was dead in seconds. Quang turned on hearing the grunt noise of his wife's last breath and saw Pat lunging at him with the knife. Quang had some defensive skills and dodged the thrusting blade. He was in a state of absolute shock, but his instinct was to stay alive. Pat's aggression peaked at the same moment Quang kicked him in the groin. Pat went down in agony and Quang grabbed him in a headlock and started to choke the life out of him. As he did so he was cursing with rage in his native tongue. Pat thought his time had finally come and was gasping for his last breath, when suddenly Quang grunted and went limp. Both men fell to the floor now slippery with Ly's blood. Pat looked up and through blurry vision saw a figure standing between two bodies. Quang was dead, with a Bowie knife sticking out of his back. It was then that a familiar voice said,

'What the hell is going on here Uncle Pat?'

Harvey was no stranger to violence and helped Pat clean up the mess. Strangely Pat was in admiration of his nephew's coolness. He would make a great house mate.

Harvey took the old Hyundai for a drive to St Marys where an old mate at a Metal Recyclers was happy to crush the unit. He even got a $100 for his effort. While he was waiting to catch a train back to Parramatta, Pat was busy with the burial. A fresh new garden in the back yard was an easy dig for a burial plot. The Phams had planned for a tropical garden, reminiscent of the Vietnamese jungles they had left so many years ago. Unceremoniously he bound Quang and Ly together face to face with duct tape. He then covered the bodies with a bag of lime that Harvey had picked up from the local hardware store. As a measure of putting his past life behind him, Pat wrapped the bodies up in his old swag. He would not need to sleep rough again in his life. As a parting gesture to the Pham's generosity for their help in his retirement plan, Pat also did some gardening. It was more out of the need for concealment, until the lime did its body devouring work, than it was for the Pham's worthy lives. He took the Jackfruit and Jambu saplings that Quang and Ly had readied for planting and placed them like headstones on the couple's final resting spot.

When Harvey finally arrived back at his new home, Pat

was staring out the back window, thinking how peaceful the sunset was. His words summed up his lack of empathy,

'How about a drink Harvey, and don't forget it's my treat for dinner tonight?'

CHAPTER 12

School Re-Union

Mary's life was made rich by helping others. She had faith in people, this was reflected in the way she found staff to assist her in the running of the café, it was a real multi-cultural group. Some she employed via word of mouth from friends and others from job placement centres. At the same time, she was just as likely to offer a job to someone from the local soup kitchen that she supported on a regular basis. Presently she had a staff of four. The assistant manager Aisha was born in Iran, she was efficient smart and a major help. The chef Marty was from Peru, he was a fourth-year apprentice and had a wondrous short order selection. There was a casual waitress named Kelly from Ireland who was very personable and well-liked by most patrons and then there was Blaze. He was hired to help with stock and cleaning. Blaze was trouble with a capital T. Mary met him at the Lions club soup kitchen and took him under her wing.

Having a reliable assistant manager allowed Mary to have some Mondays and Tuesdays off. Despite being her day off Mary spent most Tuesdays organizing food and support for the weekly Lions Club sausage sizzle at Prince Alfred Park.

In 1797 a thatched roof, log timber jail was built on the site. As the new colony's second lock-up it was built to house the idle, the worthless and the petty offenders from the local area. Timber was not a great idea for a jail, it lasted two years before the inmates made a Christmas bonfire out of it and turned it into the Village green. The next prison was made of sturdier stuff, sandstone, and it still stands north-west of the green. Today, the green is a Memorial Park named after the Royal Prince Alfred. It is the site of local ethnic festivals, occasional weddings, and soup kitchens.

As if shadowing their sad history of want and need, the present-day idle street wanderers get a feed and company from helping hands such as Mary. It was a cold blustery day when Blaze walked into Mary's life and heart. He had a story to tell, and Mary was a good listener, but Blaze was damaged goods.

Some seventies hippy mum's, that named their baby boomer kids Sky and Sundance, would look on today's dotcom 'baby bonus' Mums with disdain and perhaps envy. Disdain would be targeted at the selfish me-too attitudes and envy at their freedom. Of course, there are other superficial differences, such as today's Mum's were more likely to name their out of wed-lock off-spring, after their 'Tagger' boyfriends. This is most likely how Blaze Kennedy got his name.

At the tender age of fifteen, Blaze had a street-smart mouth and attitude to burn. In a strange ironic twist, he took it upon himself, as a bit of a loner in the world of so-called street art, to choose as his graffiti tag 'John', just to be different. Around Parramatta on all the walls that people see, filtered with scribble in Arabic or Asian hieroglyphics, the name 'John' stood out like a super tag slap in the face. To Mary he was worthy of help, and they had something in common as well, his grandmother was half Aboriginal. He was keen as mustard when she offered him a start at the Café. She had no idea of his artistic side.

Mary had done a wonderful job setting up for the 'Arthur Phillip' class of sixty-nine school reunion. Finger-food and BYO was the order of the day and Billy Chan had made available, free of charge, a selection of his best sausage wonders. It was a mild summer evening. A bright orange sunset in the west was balanced by a soft full moon, rising in the east. Anne, with the help of some friends, had decked out Mary's Café with all the old school memorabilia they could muster. They had the old jail-bird red and white striped uniforms, old school ties, badges, and trophies. They even managed to find a schoolteacher. Good old Mr Summerfield, who we all thought was old when he taught us science. Now he did not look a day older than the rest of the gathering. The treat of the night was an Australian 'Movie-tone' flick, made for the ABC, on school swimming lessons at Parramatta's newly built swimming complex adjacent to the original Cumberland Football grounds. It depicted a fair few of the gathered re-unionists in their budgie smugglers and bright pleated two-piece bikinis pouncing around with skinny bodies and smiles like movie stars.

When Jake and Anne arrived, twenty or more guests were already there. Jake gazed around the group of aged faces unable to recognize a soul. At first, he thought there may have been a mix up on the school year. That was until 'Willy the Kraut' spoke. It was like looking down a vortex of time. One by one all these work weary senior baby boomers came into focus. Lying in wait behind the shadow board of their youthful perception lurked the craggy old face of father time. But still Jake remembered them all, Jimmy Myxomatosis and Brian Stinks were still the class clowns, and the village idiot Trev Turner was a millionaire.

'No way!' thought Jake, thinking back to Trev's former 'Dunce in the Corner' status.

They made their way over to Bob and Helen, seated in the corner dressed in re-made stretched to fit High school uniforms, they looked like Tweedle-dee and Tweedle-dumb on a school excursion.

Straight up, Jake asked the question,

'Ok Helen what's the surprise?' Knowing full well they were wearing it.

'Hi bob, what's the latest on Marvin?'

'Still no reports Jake, he's just vanished!'

'Yeah, I spoke with Bill and Fritz last Saturday. They have seen nothing odd, but that Detective Moffitt apparently gave Fritz the run around and no doubt picked up on his distaste for people of other races. I heard you had a robbery at the barn.'

'You will get the firsthand report as soon as those two punching bag soaks arrive. They should be here any moment.'

'Lose anything of value?'

'A nineteenth century handmade rum jug, it was worth about three hundred dollars, but I can't put a price on my temper. Truth is Jake, I am glad the boys didn't get severely injured, other than getting beaten up by some collectors of fine art, they remained sober for a whole weekend. When I found them in the barn on Sunday afternoon, they were a sorry sight. So, I'll go easy on them tonight.'

The night moved on, in a mix of old gags and charm. It had the air of a war dance to pending retirement or worse, death. But most people over fifty are still fifteen in the mirror and the chiropractors would re-adjust the superficial dancing wounds over the following week. Everybody appeared to enjoy themselves. Especially it seems, Steve, who was last seen wondering off down the path towards the dam wall holding hands with Cheryl Mathews.

'That's great!' said Anne, as her and Jake hopped in a cab. 'Cheryl's been keen on him for a year.'

Some single people, hurt from past failures, spend the rest of their lives searching for perfection. Others wait it out in a lonely existence of social islanding, hoping the love brick of chance falls from an unknown source. The majority mix their daily grind of chores and career expectations with the occasional lustful encounter and hope. At the end of this spectrum of sad loneliness, there are characters like Steve. They float down life's drains always looking back to what might have been. They are oblivious to a world full of other people craving for company. Cheryl listened to Steve's diatribe of past destruction with fading empathy. When he finished explaining the shock and horror of finding his ex-wife spread eagled on the lounge room floor with two men from her gym, Cheryl could take no more.

'Steve?' She said with detached indifference. 'Move on mate! Get a life! Let's go for a walk and find some passion.'

Steve was dumb struck; he had never met anybody who took control of his heart strings with such precision. The hand of lust and the promise of love helped him step out of his drain of isolation. He smiled, held her closer and with all the charm he could muster told her he liked her. She responded in kind, and they walked off down the winding path towards the dam wall to the sound of guinea fowl splashing in the reeds.

Steve was now on a euphoric high, there were feelings erupting within him that made him realise he was not past his use by date. They sat on a park bench under a lamp adjacent to the boat ramp, quietly staring at each other. He gently pushed Cheryl's soft auburn hair to the side exposing her white perfumed neck. Steve sensed that there was no reluctance in her. She had also longed for new romance and ego's selfish glow that accompanied it.

'Where will all this lead?' She whispered in Steve's ear.

'To a more comfortable venue I should hope.' He smirked.

'Is that your place or mine?' She laughed.

He looked at her with the eye of lust, grinned and passionately kissed her.

'Looks like my place!' She responded as their lips parted.

Steve felt her suddenly stiffen and saw distraction in her eyes.

'What's that?'

Steve looked to where she was pointing. In the dim moon glow a large lump of material with white appendages was bobbing on the concrete lip of the boat ramp. Whatever the object was it was out of place. A closer inspection revealed what their first thoughts failed to accept; it was a headless torso. Cheryl screamed in horror; their moment of passion ended with a visual nightmare. Steve held her close and as her trembling subsided, he dialled triple zero. Fritz heard the commotion and came over to investigate. As the three of them stood there staring, not wanting to face the obvious, Fritz spoke in unison with the approaching siren.

'Odds-on Steve, that's your missing mate.'

Steve said nothing and held Cheryl closer. An hour later the area was alive with flashing lights and cops. Plain clothes detectives and forensic people had fished out the body. Moffitt, one of the first on the scene had the torso's wallet in his hand and headed over to Steve and Cheryl, making a passing comment to Fritz,

'Don't go anywhere! I'll talk with you later.'

Moffitt was calm and respectfully suggested they take a seat.

'The deceased is a Mohamed Khan, do either of you know him?'

Steve went white as reality set in.

'That's Marvin, we reported him missing this week, some of the guys from the pub thought he went to Melbourne.'

'Yes, I know I had made some preliminary checks after Bob Stickles put in a missing person report. One thing I do know for certain now is that this investigation gets stranger by the minute.'

'Who would do something like this to Marvin, he was a

real gentle bloke, wouldn't harm a fly,' winced Steve.

'Who or maybe what it was?' Moffitt responded. 'His neck wasn't cut off it was chewed off!'

The following Sunday morning Jake was walking on the north side of the lake thinking about Marvin's demise. Steve had called in the early hours of the morning with the horrific news. The Police had taped off a crime scene near the boat ramp and the media were having a field day. Mary's Café was packed with media people and nosey locals.

Jake stepped over a fallen tree that was half rotten, it had a termite mound devoid of life, somehow growing at its base. He was always fascinated by these structures, there was never any sign of movement, but still they grew and self-repaired. Nearby, a sandstone outcrop jutted out over the lake, adjacent to a large She-oak tree. A thick rope swing was attached to one of its branches and it hung out over the water. Two joggers, a mountain bike rider and a lady walking her scabby poodle, talking to it like a child, were all heading Jake's way on the track ahead.

Just to the west of the tree swing Jake could hear wood ducks squawking in a feeding frenzy. A fallen tree obscured his view of the commotion but as he approached the lake's edge, he could see what at first, he believed to be a soccer ball. The spherical object was partially hidden by lily pads and reeds. To Jake's horror, the patches of black and white were tassels of hair and bleached skin. A gut-wrenching smell of death hit him at the same time. His revulsion grew at the realisation that this chewed off head was that of his friend Marvin. Jake threw his heart up and broke out into the cold sweat of shock.

In the few minutes he took to settle, the lady with the poodle came to his aid. Her dog was barking in hysterics at a movement in the lake. Jake and the lady gazed in further horror as a pole size eel momentarily broke the surface and then disappeared into the deep water at the edge of the dam wall.

All the screaming and barking got the attention of Fritz, who was picking up rubbish on the other side of the lake. Jake yelled out for him to call the police. Within five minutes Jake could see the officers approaching from the first crime scene. Another crime scene was set up around the area. A half hour later Moffitt and his mate arrived. While Debono took a statement from the poodle lady, Mrs Barker, Moffitt spoke with Jake.

'Are you ok to talk Jake? I know this is a pretty awful thing you've seen.'

'Yeah, mate I'm starting to settle a bit, it's not every day you see a dead mate's head and a giant eel.'

'We will have our forensic team look at it, but I do find it hard to believe an eel is the killer here, I've never heard of such a thing.'

'Me neither Moffitt, but I have heard about this eel before. Billy Chan has been losing gear to it for years, he calls it Elvis, and it's nearly a pet.'

'Not a trained one I hope!'

'No, it's more a hobby. Bill sits over there in front of the Café every other day fishing for relaxation. He catches the occasional eel or carp and generally lets them go.'

'I'll bet he puts them in his tasty sausages for added flavour Jake.'

'I hope you're wrong on that one Moffitt.' Jake smiled, now starting to relax a little.

'Anyhow we will be getting some police divers in to search for more evidence and maybe they'll find the eel as well. By the way Jake, Bob told me about a run-in between Marvin and a bloke called Harvey Maitland. Can you shed any light on the matter?'

'I heard that he gave poor Marvin a hard time about being a Muslim, but I don't think they come to blows over it. Marvin was always a polite easy-going bloke, wouldn't harm a butterfly.'

'Yeah, well between you and me Jake, I don't think the eel had it in for him either, but that Maitland might be a different matter, he has a bit of an unsavoury history.'

'Did Bob tell you I seen him walking around here last week, and talking to a strange bloke at the racecourse?'

'Yeah, Bob mentioned that what did the stranger look like?'

'He was a real cool looking dude with a black ponytail. If anything, he looked a bit like an up market Columbian drug runner, if you know what I mean.'

'I sure do, as I said to Bob it sounds like Rick Hassan is hunting for staff again. Thanks Jake, that's interesting. While we are on the subject of strange Jake, what do you know about the park caretaker Fritz?'

'He keeps to himself most of the time, but he is a hard worker Moffitt. He is also a bit xenophobic, but I doubt he could be a suspect, you know the worldly type, seen it all, nothing surprises him.'

'I get the drift, but every third rock hides a spider! You best be heading home now and I 'll give you a ring if something comes up. By the way Jake, I may have to get you in to identify Maitland if I bring him in for questioning, is that ok

'No problem mate, just give me a call.'

The Parramatta Advisor was always quick to highlight a story with an eye-catching statement. Today's front-page edition lived up to the tradition.

'GIANT KILLER EEL LURKS IN LAKE PARRAMATTA'

The Police media officer had asked all the media to settle down any speculation until the coroner's report came back, but it is hard to hold a good story down. The Parramatta Leagues Club were also cashing in on the attention. Their aggressive eel icon suddenly came to life with new meaning. Tee shirt sales and memorabilia went through the roof. The pre-season competition was only a few months off, and all the footy heads were saying this was a sign of the big win ahead. Next year will be their year now that there is a real EEL to fear!

There was also talk of capturing the beast and keeping it in a glass tank in the club's foyer. Environmentalist's would not have a bar of this and pursued a capture and release strategy. Fishermen flocked to the lake to capture the 'Beast' but luckily were turned back by the Environment Protection Agency and the Local Council, latitude was shown only to known locals. Mary's Café was doing a roaring trade. She had to purchase more tables and chairs and put on additional staff. Even the world media were asking questions and CNN had done a feature on 'Nessie Down Under'. Tourism to Australia's first settlement Parramatta was taking on a new focus. The Politicians had smiles on their faces and local businesses were seeing dollar signs.

While all this was going on Moffitt continued to ask questions. He had a different agenda, and he was closing in on some two-legged suspects. Billy Chan was asked by the council ranger not to fish in his usual spot, so he started fishing at the north end of the Lake. It suited him to be out of the way of people for a while. He needed time to think, things were changing in his life and his normal jovial attitude was waning. By chance, a local reporter spotted Billy and asked some questions about the lake and the eels. The next addition of the local Advisor had a front-page grab titled,

"LAKE MONSTER NAMED AS ELVIS THE EEL.'

All the papers and news articles started to contain pieces on Parramatta's past, not just on its Rugby league status, but its people, its history, and its diversity. The 'Mouse Roared' with excitement. Australians of all cultural backgrounds sat up and started to think about Parramatta. These thoughts led to the recognition of its place as the second steppingstone in our Nation's story. It became the talking point at most outings.

'The time had finally come for Governments to recognise the areas valuable history.' The paper editorials stated.

Parramatta, the forgotten Cinderella of Sydney, was on its way. A simple focal point, a mystery, or a murder it did not matter now, the colony's history was about to be revived. The new talk around town was an injection of State and Commonwealth funds. Ideas were focussed on Parramatta's 'Cradle of the Nation' status. Restoration of nature's diversity around the lake could be made a priority with fencing to keep feral animals out and the re-introduction of quolls, bandicoots, and other natives to balance and restore the biodiversity. A Botanical Garden in Parramatta Park and a restoration of the Governor's Aviary and Observatory were now not just dreams, but possibilities. It was also time the historic precinct around the Old Female Factory and the Cumberland Mental facilities were revamped, relabelled, and had serious restoration work.

At the same time, the 'History Walk' needed to be completed from the historic Lennox Bridge along the river to a grand entrance portal that could become Parramatta's own 'Rocks District'. This could include a true impression of what made this Nation great, a museum to the men and women, the average people, the aboriginal, the convict, the soldier, the free settler, the entrepreneurs and of course the continuing flow of new immigrants. These and other ideas seemed to flourish, the regions ancestral vision was revitalised and finally the glass slipper began to fit.

CHAPTER 13

Mates

As Jake stared into the red-hot embers of the dwindling campfire misty thoughts flowed. Memories always contained subtle changes to fact. The subconscious mind had ways of building pain by-passes and pleasure parallels on the railway tracks of life. He was thinking about Marvin's funeral. To most of the blokes that attended it was a strange and surreal experience. Marvin's cousin Ahmed came up from Melbourne and together with the local Mosque, arranged for the burial at Rookwood cemetery.

Out of respect for Islamic teachings and a quick burial, the Coroner and Police conducted their forensic examination as fast as possible. It was a very solemn internment, and few words were spoken. Ahmed and the local Imam had washed the body and wrapped him in a white cloth called a Kaftan. Ahmed asked all present to refer to Marvin by his true name Muhammad. By their law only men from the Mosque and Ahmed could accompany the body to the burial site. The rest of Marvin's mates stood in quiet respect at the courtyard, where the funeral prayers had been spoken.

From a distance the whole group witnessed Muhammad's body lowered into the ground. Their collective sadness was noticeable. Strangely, a dark cloud momentarily blocked out the sun, this stamped the moment in everyone's memory. When the burial ended all turned and walked away, there were no flowers, as is customary to Muslim beliefs and there would be no headstone. In his faith our Marvin would now find peace with his God. Memories of his life and worth would now be continued by those who knew him.

Bob had wished to say a few words but held them back, there would be time for that at the non-Islamic wake that had been planned at the Rose and Thorn that afternoon. It would be the group's way of sending off a mate.

It had been two weeks since Marvin's wake. It was Bob's idea to arrange the camp out for one night at the lake, a sort of tribute to Marvin. Fritz had cleared a grassed area not far from the old road that was built back in the 1880 depression. Around the perimeter of the lake there were a lot of sandstone walls and tracks. They were the result of a government plan to keep locals in work during tough times. Today they were covered with time's blanket of soil and scrub. They also provided great living quarters for river dragons and red-belly black snakes.

It had been two weeks since Marvin's wake. It was Bob's idea to arrange the camp out for one night at the lake, a sort of tribute to Marvin. Fritz had cleared a grassed area not far from the old road that was built back in the 1880 depression. Around the perimeter of the lake there were a lot of sandstone walls and tracks. They were the result of a government plan to keep locals in work during tough times. Today they were covered with time's blanket of soil and scrub. They also provided great living quarters for river dragons and red-belly black snakes.

Earlier in the evening the boys had sat around the campfire reminiscing on the past and focusing on some of the funny stories from the locals at the Rose and Thorn. Bob spoke of Marvin's story since coming to Australia. All were saddened to think of a life so full of potential being cut short in such a way. Jake had done some research on what life was like in Kabul at the time of the Russian invasion in 1980. The spoke of the suffering that Marvin's family went through under their rule and the constant fighting in that war torn land. On a lighter note, Mick and Steve went on about being locked up in the emporium again, but this time the run-in with shop lifters had blown out into a full-scale battle. Truth fades with the time it takes for a story to evolve. Bob brought the facts back to life and the night marched on with a few beers and a billy or two of tea. Even Jim Booth turned up. He is a part-time mate and a local councillor, always attending meetings or lunches with the hob-knobs in town. He gets a bit of stick off the boys because he is one of those soft talkers, so if you do not wish to miss a hot bit of gossip you have to listen hard. The boys all marvelled that old Bob could still throw a 'Murrumbidgee Roll' with the billy. He also cooked his special damper that Mick and Steve scoffed down like a couple of starving refugees. It was a clear night, and the stars were like glow worms on the vast black ceiling above. Conversations with friends acted like a buffer against the size of things. If it were not for the village mentality our insignificance in the scheme of all things would drown our will to survive.

Bob was now snoring away, and the others faded off

to sleep talking about what they were going to have for breakfast at Mary's Café. Steve had a whinge about the hard ground and how he might sneak off to Cheryl's warm bed, Mick chuckled and mumbled something about Steve and Boothy farted.

'Did you say something Jim?' Steve asked. Then it was quiet.

Jake was looking back at past camping adventures. His parents always took the family camping down to Windang back in the early sixties. Jake continued the excitement with his own family but chose less populated further afield camp sites. One thing they all had in common were the magic textures that aroused memories. Like the smell of sand through a beach towel or the sound of rain falling on a canvas ceiling.

In the previous chapter of his life Jake's girlfriend was a fiery Irish red head named Brenda. When they met, she had two kids of her own and he had custody of his two. Their 'Brady Bunch' of pain and pleasure lasted ten years. There were good times like camping holidays and picnics, but for every happy moment there was a balancing act of setbacks. Life was a constant court case of bickering over the handouts of love or punishment to the step-kids. This coupled with real court and animosities over settlements with previous partners drove wedges into their vision of family bliss. A new house, steady income and great holidays were not enough glue to keep the bliss from blistering.

In all this there were adventures and as Jake dozed off, he was thinking of life experiences well worth documenting. Camping with four children in a five-man tent, with the weather extremes of an Australian summer had to be one of them.

Early in the summer of 1990, Jake's newly formed family were all looking forward to five glorious days of fun in the sun and roughing it on the turf at sub-tropical Scotts Head, just south of Macksville in N.S.W. The personality profiles of the children, three boys and one girl between the ages of four and eleven, had to be taken into consideration. Due to the 'Brady Bunch' family scenario, it appeared that the kid's whole existence, during wide awake moments, was purely dependent upon a system of equal shares. Not only in the quantities of food and love, but other more prominent issues such as time near the window in the rear seat of the car, time in the front seat, time in the top bunk, time in the bottom bunk and so on and so on. Of course, not being trained psychologists the adults had to ad-lib on the more aggravating points of their internal and external conflicts. It must have certainly made for interesting conversation under the canvas of the neighbouring campers. This was made obvious by the occasional curt nod and looks of pity that were shown throughout the ordeal.

On arrival at Scotts Head, it was pitch black and the children were starving. The excitement of the adventure shone through in an aura about their cute little faces. This provided just enough light to have the tent erected and the campsite in a semblance of order by about midnight. The fact that the rain held off was a godsend. The obvious presence of fruit bats, made known to all by their smell and deposits, helped provide the children with some distraction from their growling tummies.

Jake and Brenda had nicknames for the children. Firstly, there was 'Guinness' the four-year-old boy Ralf, he was named after a morbid Irish fellow on a beer commercial. His favourite habit in the share stakes was demanding the same amount of food as everyone else and then not touching a thing on his plate, probably because in his own mind he thought nobody liked him. Then there was 'Agro', Dirk, ADHD without a doubt, the eight-year-old boy, with a constant grin and the 'what's next' mentality, his share always ended up with more on him than in him. Next was 'Pugsley', Stan the nine-year-old, not named for any existing obesity problem, but what was feared may become one in the future. He somehow equated that the more he ate the more he was loved. He could consume a 1000-calorie meal with coke at MacDonald's and still request a thick shake for the road. The fear was that this was somehow linked to Jake and his mother Karen's bust up.

Finally, there was Lisa, the eleven-year-old girl. She had many aliases, from 'little miss goody two-shoes' to 'niggles with giggles' she loved to eat all the meat on her plate but had the unusual habit of hiding the good stuff like veggies under tissues, as if it wouldn't be noticed. While being helpful sometimes, she seemed to take extreme sadistic pleasure in annoying any of the unsuspecting boys.

All was well in camp. The tents were up, and everything seemed to be in order. The children were snug in their sleeping bags, their little tummies were filled with chips and coke, and it was only 1.00 am. Then came that most pleasurable part of the day, when the adults could close their eyes and dream of the times when they used to have eight hours of sleep.

6.05 am and 'Guinness' awoke!

A decision was made earlier on a simple meal strategy for the sake of sanity, so breakfast was quickly put away. Vegemite on toast was generally the first course followed by the treat of the day, 'Coco pops' a rather sugary cereal from a health point of view. However, to the children it was chocolate gold. Again, the share stake syndrome came into play, as they managed to consume one whole 600-gram box. Luckily, they left just enough milk for a cup of tea.

Next the beach! What a beauty, sun drenched, crystal clear water and a minimum of people, but before the fun could start the sunscreen had to be applied. Just mentioning the subject brought about a full range of conversation topics like, how hot the sun was that year and the hole in the ozone layer. With this came the background comments, like 'doesn't he realise how hard it is to put this stuff on when he's covered in sand?' Once this ritual was over the boys put on their new wet suits and hit the waves. Expensive Christmas presents were somehow part of the new family deal. It was strange boiler suit fashion in 30-degree temperatures but being cool was not as important as looking cool.

Meanwhile 'Niggles' and 'Guinness' frolicked by the water's edge as the holiday mood started to kick in. At this point one would think it was time to relax and ponder life's pleasures, by dreaming of island escapes and self-indulgent thoughts. Alas the responsibility of parenthood meant that one eye was always scanning the waves. It was on the lookout for disappearing heads and waving arms, while one ear was always tuned in to the background din of children's laughter and joys throughout yet another great Australian summer.

In looking back Jake realised that the good memories far outweighed the bad. But one observer's fact is often the other observer's fiction. Perhaps Brenda saw things differently when she chose to end the relationship, perhaps it had more to do with the kids than the couple, perhaps she did Jake a big favour, although it did not seem that way at the time. Despondency took hold and for a while he felt like an inland river during a drought, the dead fish of his spirit was left jumping about in the last dirty watering hole of his soul. In what seemed a heartbeat of time it was all over, the legal deals were completed, the adult kids left Jake an empty nester. He sat in a house, now empty of furniture and love. On the bright side he still had his humour and the love of his kids. It was time to move on, fifty was around the next corner and so was Anne.

The night was dark and still. The dull chorus of snores aroused Jake from a dream state. Nearby a tree branch fell and Jake looked out the tent at the reflecting light on the lake's mill pond calm. For a moment Bob and Micks choir of sleep noise faded and a dog barked in the distance. On the edge of Jake's hearing, he could just make out the mumbled resonance of talk. As he concentrated on the talk his curiosity had him crawl from the tent and slowly walk in the direction of the now obvious conversation between two men. The chat seemed to be coming up from the ground in the direction of a section of thick forest off the main track near an overhanging rock platform. Jake thought he saw a torch light flash but as he approached the scent of a nearby Melaleuca caused him to sneeze. The talking ceased immediately. Jake stood there for ten minutes and heard nothing, but the stop starts snoring from the camp. With his senses now heightened Jake turned to go and wake his mates, in that instant he lost consciousness.

A couple of warbling crows had most of the campers stirring early. Bob was first up and had the billy on for his morning cuppa and toast. He looked over to Jake's tent and noticed the flap was open and his empty sleeping bag half out. The smell of the toast had the rest of the blokes up and about in minutes, one night out on hard ground was all the wilderness experience required for most people in their age group. Mick wandered off to relieve himself and while in the process he noticed with a shock Jake lying face down some fifty metres from the camp. Bob called the Ambulance and Mick called the Police. Jake had come around but was still groggy by the time the Ambulance arrived. He had an egg the size of a cricket ball on the back of his head and no doubt a bit of concussion. Anne was called and met them all at the Hospital. To the relief of all, he was released later that day and told to take a couple of days off work. The police scoured the area and were unable to find any indication or reason for the attack on Jake. To Moffitt it was just another piece of a puzzle that he was determined to fit.

Later, that week, another couple of mates had a meeting at a nearby location. One was wagging school and one was wagging work. Blaze was meant to be cleaning the tables at Mary's Café, but the hot afternoon and the cool water offered too much temptation. Mustafa held a school suspension warning letter in his hand contemplating his next move. If his dad saw it, he would be grounded for a month.

'School sucks!' he thought, 'so what if I didn't show up at

school for a few days, the teacher's don't give a crap.'

For a moment he worried about the punishment, it was not old pig-head Maclean the year-master that bothered him, it was his old man's leather strap.

He knew this would be his last warning, 'so what!' He thought, 'Tomorrow's another day.'

His decision was made, he screwed the note up and as he stuffed it in a log, he heard Blaze calling from the rope swing.

'Come on Mustard it's your turn.'

Mustafa liked the way Blaze treated him, even being called Mustard gave him a sense of inclusion.

CHAPTER 14

Tribal thoughts

The overhang rock jutted far out over the lily encrusted billabong. Over generations the tribe had carved its soft sandstone surface and as such it was a special place for spiritual and ceremonial gatherings. Gilpani stood proud on the rock's ledge awaiting the return of the elders. He was silhouetted by a full moon to the east and brooding storm clouds to the west. Clutching his hand-made spear and resplendent in his tribal colours, he was an icon to his culture. The creek that had formed the billabong was flowing free and fast from the previous night's storm. There was a fresh breeze blowing from the south and occasionally Gilpani could smell the fires from the camp below the overhang, and the roasting eel in the ceremonial ground-oven on the ridge.

The area on which Gilpani stood had been cleared of bark and leaves. His eyes now focused on the exposed carved effigy of the Dreamtime Eel. Over the years of their history this tribal serpent had witnessed all the male rites of passage, and now it meandered across the expanse of this sandstone slab, alive in spirit and mystery. Gilpani could not help but be reminded of the great eel that he had caught to make the ritual feast for his journey to manhood. The elders were now gathering on the forest side of the carving. Some of the warriors were preparing the coloured ochres and pouring it onto the body of the serpent. Others were removing the cooked eel from the ritual ground-oven and preparing it for the feast.

A lightning strike failed to disturb any of the gathered men. The cloud burst left Gilpani wet and glistening in moonlight reflected rain. He was propped up by his spear and stood still on one leg, his right foot squarely mounted above his left knee. His eyes wept a little as the white and red ochres of the ritual paint trickled down the side of his face. Through blurry vision Gilpani saw the Elder sharpening the sacred bone. His stomach turned with nerves as he was beckoned forward to step across the serpent and onward to manhood, and the feast of welcome. After the scarring ceremony was performed, two delicate brow cuts now wept with the blood of a new warrior of survival.

The hourglass of sand flowed on. Over time a new age warrior of the Law, stood in the shadow of Gilpani on the rock's ledge, his name was Moffitt. The creek was no longer there. It was replaced by a man-made dam and the ancient carving was well hidden by eons of storm and tempest.

Moffitt was a deep thinker and a man of minimal talk. He had been standing on the large outcrop of sandstone for about an hour, running facts and associations through his mind. There was a turn of weather in the air, but the heat was still stifling. He had gone over all the names, places and deeds of people and things in this recent case and had concluded that there was more than one act to the story. Three names stood out with menace, Hassan, Maitland, and Fritz, the first two for criminality, the latter for racial hate. Three other names in the investigation offered help in putting the puzzle together, Billy Chan, Mary, and Jake. There was also the reason he stood at that very location, the place where Jake received a headache two nights earlier. Moffitt walked to the edge of the rocky outcrop to a point where the root of an Ironbark took a right-angle bend towards the water. Some inconsiderate polluters had recently deposited an empty VB longneck and a snickers wrapper. Both were partially hidden by leaf litter but new enough to take back to the Lab.

A flutter of wings caught Moffitt's attention; a cockatoo had perched himself on a branch of an old Banksia. With its grey tongue hanging loose, as testament to the day's heat, its bright yellow crown suddenly erupted as Moffitt spoke.

'Polly wants a beer. You read my thoughts mate.'

The cockie's bulging eyes followed Moffitt's movements as he donned a set of rubber gloves and placed the rubbish into a forensic bag. It was a long shot, but a worthy print could bring this caper to a head. He then walked off down the trail with the Cocky screeching in phase with his thoughts. It was time to ask Billy the butcher some questions about eels and other slippery creatures.

CHAPTER 15

Billy and Elvis the Eel

Billy could see from the amount of light filtering through the old, faded curtains that it was a dull day. It matched his mood. He was sitting on the edge of his unmade bed and staring out the window. His thoughts fragmented.

'The lawns need mowing... I thought she would at least call... stuff the lawns I might go fishing...she has been gone a week... what does she want, I have a business to run... I give her everything she asks for... look at that bloody clover it looks like the bindies are losing the battle...'

He fell back on the bed and dozed off into a depressive dream laden sleep, the only escape he had. A loud knock at the door brought Billy back.

'Coming, give us moment!' He yelled.

It was Moffitt.

'Billy Chan, isn't it? I'm Detective Moffitt from Parramatta, could I ask you a few questions about this Lake Parramatta death?'

Moffitt did not miss much; Bill's house was a mess. He was also despondent in nature and had sadness in his eyes. The observant cop knew all the signs. Wife problems, it was written all over Bill's face.

'Certainly, mate, come in excuse the mess, the wife is taking a short break.'

'Thanks Bill, I think I know you? I have been to your shop once or twice. If I remember rightly, you make a rather good snag.'

'Yeah, I like to please the customers, makes for a good retirement one day. I know you too, seen you walking into Parramatta a few times.'

'It can be a small place to some and a lonely place to others I guess, that's why I like to walk, the more you see the more you know. Your mate Jake told me you might be able to help fill in some gaps about this giant eel and other matters of interest concerning lake life.'

'I go to the lake for a bit of peace and quiet detective, I see things, but I like to keep to my own business and let others keep to theirs. I have a couple of good butchers working for me now and I manage to get down there a few times a week. Although lately I have not been going as much, you know family issues.'

'That's fine Bill, but any thing you can recall about strange activity could help us solve this recent death. First up tell us about this giant eel?'

'Oh, I've been losing tackle to that land locked monster for years. I call him Elvis, because just when you think he has passed on or moved on, he pops up to give me a bit more fishing excitement. Of course, I never catch him. He is too old and smart for that. Even if I did, I think I would let him go. You know what I mean, how could anyone eat an old friend.'

'Yeah, I see your point Bill, but could that old friend of yours attack one of us?'

'I doubt it detective, that's all-media hype and bullshit. As I said he has been around a long time and in that time, with kids and dogs swimming every other day, don't you think there would be a stack of reports by now?'

'My thoughts exactly Bill, that's why I'm interested in strange human behaviour, Elvis may be an innocent who just copped a free meal, and his only guilt was disturbing the scene of a crime.'

'Well, there are a few odd types that pass by me occasionally, take Fritz for instance. He is a bit of a racist, but he has never done me any harm. He seems to show an interest in keeping the Lake and Café area in good order and he is Mary's stepbrother. She is a great lady who would not put up with too much of his racism, especially around her multi-cultural staff. Just between you and me she has his measure.'

'Yes, I have had a coffee there and she seems to run a tight ship, is there anything else?'

'I put on a free feed of snags at the shop on Wednesday's for local seniors and a few of the intellectually disabled people from the Cumberland facility. A couple of them do come via the Lake track, but they wouldn't hurt a fly.'

'Can I have their names Bill?'

'One is a funny little guy called Vince, he's always in his pyjamas. He walks alone and does not talk much. You know the type, arm up to wave, head bowed away from you, no eye contact, an increase in speed and a muffled 'Hi

Bill' as he passes. Another bloke who calls himself Golly is the complete opposite, always stops and smiles. He does not say much, just asks if I caught the big one today. He is a gentle giant. Stands about two metres tall, has that curious look about him. He eats well though, always has a couple of pieces of fruit in his pockets. I even showed him how to rig the line once, but he lost interest quick. Apart from that there are the local kids who occasionally wag school and spend the day down at the rope swing, but that is not my problem it is theirs. I know that they graffiti around the place but what can you do, you never catch them in the act.'

'Just two last questions Bill, did you know the deceased?'

'I may have met him once with Jake and his mates down at the pub's Friday night karaoke.'

'Yes, I heard you put on a surprisingly good show as an Elvis impersonator and I can tell from talking to you, you're not a slimy Elvis like your mate in the lake.'

Detectives like Moffitt use their own eyes as information magnets. Most guilty people talk too much when stared at and he could tell from Bill's demeanour that he was an honest bloke. Still, this did not stop him asking the most important question.

'Did you kill him, Bill?'

'No detective, I couldn't even kill the cows I cut up!'

'Good answer Bill you have been an immense help. Do you mind if my mate and I pop in for a free snag occasionally?'

'Anytime you like detective.'

'By the waybill, what sort of fruit does the big fellow eat?'

'Grapefruit, he often talks about his tree at the home!'

'Well on that sour note I'll take my leave, thanks for your help Bill.'

Elvis lay dormant in the cool soft mud of his lily encrusted home with no thoughts of time or space, he just existed. Procreation seemed a distant whim within his chemistry. In truth landlocked giants like Elvis whose body clock of hormones do not switch on, can remain as females for life and this maybe the trigger for gigantism. If Billy Chan had known this, he may have named his beast Priscilla 'Queen of the Lake'.

The only two guides in life for Elvis now were hunger and rest. This did not preclude a sense of change. He felt the transient subtle turns of heat and cold, of light and dark and the vibrations caused by the movements of wind and earth. He also saw the motion of ducks and guinea fowl legs, plus occasional human, and dog swimmers. He had no name or thought for any of this, his prime driver like all species was survival. His world was awash with shades, not colours or hues. The electrical and chemical circuits of his mind had retained the experiences of lessons learnt throughout his long life. Instructions to avoid pain or danger had helped Elvis remain unconsumed, uncaptured and in human terms unforgiving in survival. He was an enigmatic leviathan imprisoned by the walls of a man-made dam, but he was always in control of his domain.

CHAPTER 16

Zephyr

It had been a month since Marvin's funeral and although Moffitt had some good clues, they were all circumstantial at this stage. The coroner came back with a 'Death by suspicious causes' tag, saying that the victim drowned after being knocked out by a blunt implement. But in summing up, said the victim's head may have hit the dam wall as he slipped into the water. There were bite and bruising marks on the right calf. This account did not let Elvis off the hook yet. Moffitt favoured the word suspicious in the report and had interviewed various people of interest. The prints were no good on the beer bottle and the one they managed to get off the snickers wrapper was an unknown on the file.

The interviews with Rick Hassan and Harvey Maitland proved to be hopeless. Both had history and knew how to manage questions. Their alibis were watertight. Harvey had matured since his last run in with the law, from a drop kick teenage loser to a smart mouth punk waiting for someone to knock his fillings out. His response was what Moffitt expected. Rick on the other hand played the role of a surprised honest businessman who could not recall who he talked to at the racetrack. The fact that he brought a Queens Council Barrister to the interview added sauce to the rotten pie, that Moffitt knew him to be. Basically, both interviews added no light to the case of Marvin's demise, but Moffitt did not let them off the hook easy. He left them with nervous thoughts that he still had something on both, and his eye contact reinforced it.

There had been no recent giant Eel sightings and life had pretty much returned to normal around the lake. Bill and Jake had not reported any suspicious strangers in the area and Fritz was proving out to be a help as well. He had reported that the graffitist 'JOHN' was back to his destructive tricks, leaving his tags in caves on the north side of the lake. He offered up as suspects some kids he caught wagging school and starting a small fire on the water's edge, down by the rope swing. He even came up with a name 'Mustafa Sadat'. Fritz was proving to be a good detective in his own right. He had found a school suspension warning letter in a hollow log close to where the boys lit the fire. It also listed the school and the teacher's name. Moffitt was keen to follow any leads, so he made an appointment with the school principal in the following week and as events unfolded it became more important.

The 'Melbourne Cup' race day was always a big event at the 'Rose & Thorn'. Moffitt and Bones were off duty and Jake had booked a table for lunch and an afternoon of fun. The pub always put on a top seafood feast, and this coupled with over-the-top betting on 'the race that stops the nation', made for a great afternoon. The place was packed with regulars and to get a table at this event you had to book months in advance. Paul the publican made sure only the freshest prawns and oysters were served, and this coupled with great lucky door prizes just added to the excitement.

Everybody thought they knew the winners and as the bets and beers flowed on, the big race moment arrived. The favourite at this stage of the day had lost its edge and most of the blokes around the table were having a late plunge on an Irish gelding at long odds. Mick had been bragging about a recent thousand-dollar jackpot he won at the Leagues club. So, the horse with a tag of 'Micks Joy' stole their attention, due in part to his joy and secondly to the horse's Irish roots, nobody seemed to care anymore about weight, track, trainers, or jockeys it was all about the 'karma' of the name. The smart ones had each way bets.

A hush went up over the crowd. Suddenly you could hear all the TV screens in the pub at once and the race caller shouting.

'They're racing, in this year's Melbourne Cup...'

Three minutes later a large cheer went up, most of the crowd would be happy, the favourite won, and 'Micks Joy' only missed out by a head. Mick bet a bundle on the nose and lost a sizable chunk of his jackpot. Bob and Moffitt cashed in, with a couple of hundred in the pocket at day's end. Steve backed the favourite and won a motza, well at least enough to shout the bar. He played it real coy and did not tell a soul how much he won, but the table could tell it was a tidy sum.

It had been another great Cup Day at the pub, now the boys were talking about the weekend ahead. The Nelson Bay wine festival was on, and Anne had booked two villas near d'Albora Marinas, right in the heart of the action.

'Hey Jake!' shouted Steve over the din of post-race excitement. 'Don't forget the dolphin and whale watch cruise out to Broughton Island, Cheryl is really looking forward to that.'

'Don't worry mate it's all taken care of, Bob's got a mate who runs a trawler up there, turns out his good golf buddy runs the cruise. That means a twenty per cent discount.'

'You beauty! What about the four of us have a round of golf at the course up there, I hear it's fairly good?'

'Don't push it Steve, our times at a premium and you should be thinking of pleasing your lady, if you know what I mean.'

'Yeah, I get ya drift Jake, I'll be 'Gentleman Jim' for the weekend, can't wait.

'Neither can I mate.'

As the fun rumbled on Moffitt got a phone call. From the grimace on his face, you could tell it was business. There had been a bush fire in the Lake reserve and a body had been found in its wake. It was a hot dry day outside and this went largely unnoticed in the air-conditioned comfort of the bar. Most of the blokes were under the weather by now so it was not till the following day that their interest peaked. Moffitt and Bones had to leave to get some sleep before an early morning start. Tomorrow was going to be another big day and they both knew it.

Slivers of flesh from a recent feast took their time to wash from Elvis's curved razor-sharp band of teeth into his gullet. He was now at rest on the mud at the bottom of his dark cavern. It was a cave that in the light of day would have revealed a pictorial tapestry in ochre of the lives of its former inhabitants, their stories, and their surviving ways. As Elvis relished this moment of eel peace his dorsal fin began to quiver. A man with abstract thoughts wrestled above. In contrast to the dark and dank cave interior, this man's world was a kaleidoscope of colour, made brighter by a day of extreme heat. However, this colourful world view went unappreciated, his was a world of amalgamated pain and pleasure. Self-absorption blinded him to his surrounds and the starting crackle of a scrub fire.

Harvey stared at the ripples on the lake's surface as he held Blaze in a suffocating head lock, occasionally tapping his skull with clenched bony knuckles.

'You stupid prick!' He scowled.

'I hope you didn't tell this Mustard any of our little secrets, you fool.'

Blaze let out a gasp, as Harvey eased off a bit.

'No honest mate, I just …just bragged a little about making a bit of extra cash.'

'Yeah! For doing what?'

'Just helping a mate out with some deliveries, no detail mate, just helping out that's all!'

'Well, I'll tell you something that might keep you breathing moron, these people I deal with don't stuff around, any sniff of trouble and you may end up in a concrete filled drum in the lake. So, keep your mouth shut from now on, and ditch this mate of yours or he could go for a swim too, got it?'

Harvey smelt the smoke and looked up to see Golly running through the bush on the other side of the lake. The fire was a fair way off to the west of the reserve, so he was not really bothered by it. They had planned for a midday meeting at the cave, but he was puzzled by Golly's haste. He had a thought that Golly may have started the fire but pressed on with the admonishment of Blaze. The quickly rising heat of the day and this little bit of exercise had caused sweat to trickle off his brow and splash on Blaze's panicky face. Harvey gave a couple more knuckle taps and pushed his fearful mate into the lake for an unrequested dip.

Elvis stirred in the mud as his flight senses kicked in. He took off at lightning speed between the two fleshy appendages that suddenly appeared. Blaze felt the rush and the rub of something large and alive go between his legs. As a ball of mud encased his body, his scream could be heard across the lake. Goliath heard the scream and ran faster. Harvey looked into Blaze's eyes and saw the fear.

'Get me out of here!' He begged in terror.

'Something bloody big just went through my legs!'

Harvey smirked at first and then remembered the eel story about Marvin. He also recalled his own encounter, at this same spot when Golly and he were kids.

'Get yourself out he yelled back at Blaze; I hope that stinking Eel eats ya!'

Blaze struggled ashore and as he looked up the fear was back on his face.

'What now?' Harvey shouted, at the same time realising that Blaze was not looking at him, but over his shoulder to the left. In the same instant there was a blur across his vision, as a boulder smashed into Blaze's stunned face and cracked his head like a watermelon. Goliath just stood there with a dumb and curious look on his face watching the colourful waves of red and brown lapping on the rocks. Blaze slipped back into the water in a whirlpool of blood and mud as the last gurgling sound of life ebbed from his mouth.

'What the hell did you do that for?' Harvey screamed.

Moffitt and Bones were up at the lake at 7.00am the following morning. It was a much cooler day and the smoke haze still lingered over the water. A flock of crows were screeching overhead as they approached the scene.

'Edgar Allen Poe territory,' Moffitt thought.

The fire area where the body had been found was taped off and secured through the night. The bush fire brigade Captain who was first on the scene had made a report that the fire had started one hundred metres southwest of where the body was found. Early speculation of the cause was ignition from a discarded cigarette butt. The fire's proximity to the rope swing had now made the Mustafa interview a priority.

There were a few curious bystanders hanging around the taped off walking track. One bloke caught Moffitt's attention due to his height, unkempt hair, and pasty look. Good detectives were well versed around crime scenes, so he had Bones get their details. It was a natural trait for certain types, especially arsonists to visit their workmanship after events. Every piece of information counted.

The body was burnt beyond recognition and the only clue was a piece of clothing on a tree branch that looked like pyjama flannel. This was the third reference to pyjamas in this area of investigation. Moffitt was careful not to be drawn into assuming the cases were linked, coincidences always played a role. He would also keep this in mind with the Mustafa interview. However, his memory of a recent conversation with Billy Chan and the story of a pyjama wearing fellow named Vince sparked interest. Just like pieces of a puzzle falling together on a thought, a call came through on the radio that a patient named Vince Smith had been reported missing from the Cumberland hospital and he was known to often walk through the reserve. Moffitt filtered the facts as he focused on the starting point of the fire. His knowledge of a certain school truant, who liked to start fires in that vicinity, was foremost in his mind. An interview with the school principal was set for the following day.

Moffitt had booked the interview with the Kings School principal at 10:30 am. It was his day off, so he decided to walk to the meeting via the Newsagent at the Oatlands shops. Moffitt was born in Dundas and his old man was a Burnside orphan, so he knew the area well. He always placed his lotto bets on a Wednesday. Lady luck did not shine that often but the trickle of money that came back once every month or so kept him in the game for a chance at the big one. He had dressed smart casual for the interview, so it was not going to be a physical walk, just a slow amble. He left home allowing plenty of time to get to the school.

He proceeded up Pennant Hills Road and crossed at the next lights. This was the intersection with James Ruse Drive, a highway that cut through the heart of Parramatta like a knife wound. As usual, for this time of day, it was choked with city bound drivers. The intersection was also the start of a run of magnificent homes built by Burns Philps and company from 1909. Sir James Burns was a Scottish born philanthropist who used his hard-earned wealth to help the orphaned children of Sydney and surrounds. The homes are all distinctive designs which allowed the children a sense of individuality. Sir

James was a great Australian who will always be remembered by the name tag 'One of Nature's Gentlemen' in the homes and gardens of the Burnside Estate. All the homes have a different name, the one that Moffitt's father had been in was called Reid.

Times have changed and part of the estate has been divided up and sold off to different religious schools and teaching establishments. Sir James's own home called Gowan Brae, now makes up part of the Kings School complex. One home is now part of another religious school complex and as Moffitt looked across the road, he noticed a huge school emblem and motto had been placed on the end wall of the building. The motto read, 'TO HEAR IS TO OBEY'. This sent a shiver down his spine, when he thought of the use those words had been put to throughout history. Whether for good or evil, in his mind the words ran contrary to human individuality and reason.

'Why not 'TO READ IS TO LEARN'?' He thought.

Moffitt walked on down the hill passed the million-dollar homes of the Burnside Garden housing estate. As a kid he once played here on paddocks that in their heyday were the fruit bowl of Parramatta. Across the footbridge at Brickfield Creek the buildings changed to a mixture of old and new. This was Oatlands proper where old housing commission homes mingled with more expensive rebuilds. He strolled on past his old school, Oatlands Public. Little had changed and he reminisced about his old teachers and mates.

'What had become of them? Old Mr Livingston was probably dead now.'

He smiled to himself remembering the day when the old bloke removed a couple of loose first teeth from this petrified future copper's mouth, seconds later he was shown the teeth in a handkerchief. Moffitt did not feel a thing other than profound respect. He went on to higher classes after that year with Livingston, some teachers are worth their weight in gold.

Halfway up the hill on Belmore Street East, Moffitt stopped at the Newsagents to put his lotto on. Down the road of the area's history this group of shops had barely changed. Super stores and markets had no impact here yet. The butcher, the veggie-man, the post office, the chemist and the milk bar were a working museum to the 1950's. Adjacent to the shops, a couple of new mac-mansions had been recently built, with skillion roofed beach house architecture, of the type that Moffitt detested.

'No room for a game of cricket in their backyards.' He thought.

Cushioned between the two was a double story housing commission red box dwelling, showing its age. This image was a metaphor to the area in general. The ever-observant Moffitt noticed the Audi on the stencilled driveway of one mansion and the remnants of a beat up Torana on a puddled weed patch in the poorer dwelling's front yard. The differences continued as he acknowledged the business suited driver of the Audi and the blonde lady owner of the Torana. Mr Audi was head down and focussed on the day ahead, while the lady was helping to fix one of her toddler's bikes. She had a cigarette in her mouth and her track-pants were at half-mast. Not a good look, but at least she returned a good morning to Moffitt, whereas Mr Audi did not bother to respond. Moffitt continued his walk towards the Oatlands golf club, now feeling a little indifferent as to the mix of wealth and character.

Percy Simpson built Oatlands House in the 1830's. Originally a sheep farm it remains today one of the earliest homes in the Parramatta district. It was thought that the name reflected the first sowing of oats in Australia, but the name was taken from Oatlands Park in England. The surrounding land is Oatlands Golf Course, which was opened in 1931. This anglicised gentleman's country club of the 1950's had changed little in recent years. With the influx of wealthy golf playing Asians from Hong Kong and Korea, competition for winnings was now shared with the aging old boys. Moffitt had the occasional game of social golf but was more excited by the nineteenth hole social aspect, than the early starts and the weather extremes.

He now turned into Ellis Street. Halfway down the street on the right-hand side stood an old nineteenth century dwelling that was probably an original farmhouse. A gaunt looking gentleman was sitting on the veranda with book in hand. He bid him a good morning which was returned with a subdued grunt. Instantly he recognised the face as one of the inquisitive onlookers on the day of the fire. He was about to continue the conversation when the gent abruptly went inside. Moffitt made a mental note to follow up with Bones and get some details on this suspicious looking character. As he walked on up the hill past the artificial creek and water falls in the Hunterford estate, he began to think on how he would handle the pending interview. The best approach would be to get the kid to reveal as much as possible with carrot and stick psychology does not force.

Moffitt dodged a convoy of B-double rigs as he crossed

Pennant Hills Road to get to the school of Kings. Most of the trucks could use the M2 motorway, but he guessed the fee was their lunch money for the drive.

Kings School is a magnificent educational facility. Private and Government money was not spared in providing these privileged students with the best of everything. There was a state-of-the-art basketball centre and sporting facilities including fifteen playing fields used for cricket and rugby union, fourteen tennis courts, seven outdoor basketball courts, seven soccer fields, two swimming pools and a diving pool. There was also a gym that came complete with an indoor rifle range. These facilities blended well with the 1910 architecture of Gowan Brae and the iconic sandstone chapel and gate house. Moffitt was still in awe as he approached the principal's office.

Mustafa sat opposite Moffitt at the principal's office table. Trickles of sweat on the boy's brow reflected his fear. His father, a local entrepreneur from the trucking industry was there also and appeared calm and thoughtful. He was a big man and well spoken, but his size and demeanour indicated a stern approach to life's problems. He was convinced there had been some sort of mix up, his son was a good boy. It was hard for Moffitt to tell who the boy was afraid of most, the police, or his dad.

One thing was obvious from the start of the interview, Mustafa had no respect at all for his year master, as he barely looked at him. Moffitt sized up the situation and decided not to be too hard on the boy. He was after information and understood this kid was just a player in the story. Political correctness was not one of this cop best attributes and what he least wanted now was a scene of aggravation that could curtail new knowledge. Moffitt smiled at all present to quell concern, at the same time he was thinking of something he just read about political correctness being the ability to pick up a dog turd by the clean end.

The detective laid out the story of the fire and the gruesome death in finer detail than that represented in the newspaper. He held back on the suspension warning letter and the earlier fire that Fritz had come across. Moffitt looked around the table with the anguish of the event on his face then stopped and stared directly at Mustafa.

'Mustafa could you tell us your whereabouts last Tuesday afternoon, as we have already established you were not at school. Your year master Mr Maclean informed me of that when I rang him earlier today.'

The boy was visibly shaken and proceeded to mumble.

'I..., I was with... my m... mate down at the pool.'

'Is that the Parramatta pool complex?'

'Yeah, yeah it was really hot, and Blaze and I met there at lunchtime.'

Looking at his father's expression of disgust, he continued.

'We were there all afternoon, I left about four and headed home, Mum would have started to get worried if I left any later.'

'Did you talk to anyone else while you were at the pool?'

'Just the pool guy, you know the cleaner guy, oh yeah and a couple of scraggy, oh I mean girls.'

His father started to flare up at his son's language, but Moffitt contained the situation and continued.

'Do you ever go down to the lake for a swim Mustafa?'

'Yeah, weekends sometimes.'

'But you have wagged school during the week as well. Haven't you? Did you go to the lake then?'

'No... I don't think so'

'Well, I know so, mate. Your suspension warning letter was found by the park caretaker on the same day he warned you about lighting a fire. Am I right?'

'Yeah, I guess so!'

'So, who is this Blaze?

'He's a kid I met down there, works at the café, he's cool man!'

Mustafa knew his biggest worry now was his dad and strangely felt more relaxed,

'What the hell!' He thought.

His father was in shock, the leather strap would be off that night, but for now he remained steady. Moffitt summed up the interview and thanked everyone for their attendance. He had retrieved another name to follow up on and would check out the pool guy for Mustafa's alibi, which would get him off the hook for the 'Melbourne Cup' day fire. His final remark to Mustafa put his thoughts into perspective.

'Keep your nose clean! Mustafa, respect for your dad, your teachers, and the Law. That should avoid us having any more of these interviews here or downtown.'

As Moffitt left the room, he could see Mustafa's father place his firm hand on his son's shoulder, the boy was in for it for sure, but hopefully out of Moffitt's radar for good. Summer was in the air and this case was warming up as well. In the weeks ahead Moffitt would need to find time for a coffee at his new favourite spot, the Lake Café and arrange for a talk with a couple of characters whose names had popped up in this investigation, one was Blaze another was supposedly a Jolly Giant.

CHAPTER 17

Breeze

Goliath was lying under his grapefruit tree when one of the carers, Eric approached him with the shocking news of his mate's demise in the bush fire. He showed concern but the carer did notice he seemed to be more bothered by the fire's damage to his forest retreat, than to his mate Vince.

Although Harvey had told him to keep quiet about all the fuss and excitement of that afternoon, puzzling thoughts were going through Golly's mind. He was trying to put the events down at the cave in some form of order but his disability and the effects of the tablet that Harvey had given him made the recollection a collage of images. He could see blood and mud. He could see the big canvas tarp that Harvey dragged out of the cave and placed the rocks on. He could even remember tying up the package and helping Harvey drag it into the cave and then push it into the water. He remembered the funny bubbles coming up as it slipped into the deep water. For some reason though, he was unable to remember what was in the bundle. But he was happy now, the day was still, and the sun shone through his tree putting shadows of leaves and fruit, now ready for picking, on to his soft green resting place.

'Harvey would be happy,' he thought, 'it was fun to trick Eric and not take the medication.'

The preliminary investigation of the lake fire forwarded to the coroner concluded that there were no suspicious circumstances surrounding Vince's death other than mis-adventure. It seemed that fear was as much the cause of death as the fire. It was a combination of a sweltering day and a tinder dry forest. When the fire was ignited carelessly by person's unknown the wind was blowing at about ten knots from the southwest. Vince had possibly shied away from the trail when he heard voices ahead of him, he most likely thought to walk around them and pick up the trail later. He was scrub bashing north-west of the fire-starting point when the fire took hold. He had apparently panicked, and tracks indicated that he started to run, not out of the fires path but with it. A rock on the ground under his head and a slight crack in his skull indicated he may have tripped while running. The smoke possibly overcame him before the fire did its gruesome work.

Jake and Anne pulled up in the driveway of 'Ravenswood' with as much excitement about being home as they had when they left for the Nelson Bay holiday. Since its pur-chase, the old family home quickly filled with the life and loves of the new owners. Their home was a place where memories were kept like hidden treasures, locked up in senses such as smell, sight and touch. It was also vis-ibly present in items such as pictures, furniture, and old memorabilia. Their memories could even be found in the scent on old clothes, conversations once spoken and, in the time, well of lounges once sat on. The images of their friends who were no longer living or of children growing and changing, hung around as the fruits of life. It was always good to come home.

Helen Stickles called the Nelson Bay festival 'a real treat' and that just about summed up the way they all felt. The festival had become a yearly pilgrimage for Jake, Anne, Bob, and Helen but this year a new pair of love birds had joined them. Steven and Cheryl were on a hormone high of discovery and everything that the six of them did over the three-day weekend blossomed in the new-lover's glow. They hired bikes for a ride to Fingal Bay, hiked up Tomaree Mountain and danced at the club till mid-night. Steve thought he had lost a few kilos, although none of the rest did and they all had sore legs for the following week. But the real treat of the trip at least for most of the group was the whale watch cruise to Broughton Island.

There were dolphins riding bow waves halfway to the Island and the sea swell was just enough to keep the passengers tummies tumbling in unison with the dolphin's antics. Although the Captain had the passengers prepared, the noise from the boats stern and the huge wash startled all on board. At first Jake thought the motor had blown, but soon the awe of the crowd revealed all. A whale had breached within twenty metres of the boat. Its gleaming white barnacle encrusted fins spread like giant wings and clapped the water with so much force that nearly everyone on board was wet with spray. Poor old Steve did not get wet, he missed the whole spectacle. He was busy below with his head in the toilet, throwing up the morning's bacon and eggs. When sea sickness hits, it generally does not let go until you are back on dry land. He was a new man on the hike across Broughton

Island and soaked up the sun along with Cheryl's caring attention, just like the talking sock on that cough medicine add. But he spent the homeward journey back to the 'Bay' on his knees once again praying to the dunny god for salvation.

Steve finally had a reprieve when the boat pulled up in the Marina at Nelson Bay. Five minutes back on dry land and he was a new man. The festival was in full swing, there were jazz, and blues bands all complimented with wine and food tasting from local businesses. Bob was happy enough getting stuck into the oysters and washing them down with his cold tea, while the rest of the crew hoed into the Hunter Valley reds. The last day was spent at the beach, Jake surfed while Bob fished, but the rest were happy to sleep it off in the sun.

The three-day holiday went too quick, but it served its purpose, a recharge for the run down to Christmas. Bob droves home to a chorus of snores with happy dreams, while Van the Man's music filtered the sounds, making the drive home almost bearable.

The Monday morning sleep-in was a bonus for both Jake and Anne after such a hectic three days. Jake rolled over to catch a few moments more shut eye, but the chatty lorikeets were announcing their arrival on the back veranda. Anne took this as her wake-up call and went out to give them a feed. She had a passion for local wildlife that almost rivalled that of the Leyland brothers. Only Anne went one step further and had names for most of the feathered visitors. Her latest sad story of loss centred on Chuckles, an ancient cockatoo, probably in his fifties, who up to a few weeks ago virtually lived on the veranda. He had a broken beak, a featherless head and was one leg short of a pair. If there was such a thing as a bird's war pension, he was a limp up start.

Another characteristic that set Chuckles apart from his clan were the strange noises he made when letting Anne know he was hungry. Jake thought it sounded like a cat on heat, with more of a howl than a 'Polly wants a cracker' garble. But old Chuckles did the disappearing act about two weeks back and Anne knew she would not see the poor old fellow again. It was on the weekend lake walk on a section of track that only a few people use that Chuckle's fate was confirmed. He was laying there dead on the track, crooked beak facing skyward. Of all places to end his days, with 360 degrees of choice, he chose to let the one who cared for him most find him. Anne cried and went on about the wonders of nature. Jake thought it was all just coincidence.

It was a crisp sunny morning, a perfect day to mow the lawns and the summer grass was screaming for a haircut. Straight after breakfast Jake headed for the garden shed, but something was not right. The shed door was partially open. The first discovery was that the lawnmower was missing the second was when Anne yelled out if he had seen the laptop. The break-in was a personal affront and both Jake and Anne could not help feeling violated in some way. The Police came the following morning, but finger printing for two items was not worth their time. There was no issue with the insurance payments. Jake had Steve come around and help with the lawns until he got a new mower, but the security in their new home had to be re-visited. Both Anne and Jake were on edge for a while and unknown visitors and hawkers had to be scrutinised.

It could be said that Patrick Maitland was partly responsible for the way his nephew Harvey turned out. Over the years he had flitted in and out of the lives of his dead brother's family, always scamming for hand-outs. No one ever talked about the other brother Ray, he was serving a life term in Long Bay Jail. So unwittingly Pat became a bit of a mentor to his wayward nephew. Harvey never could see anything wrong in Pat's behaviour, if anything he admired his sense of freedom and frivolous view of life.

Since Harvey moved in things were looking up a bit. The boy knew how to keep their little business with the Pham family secret, and it was never mentioned. The fact that Harvey always seemed to have a quid in his pocket was a bonus. Pat was starting to think of Harvey as the son he never had. A son to help him out in his old age is just what he needed.

On hearing about the good fortune of the McCooey's, who lived just down the road, snake like thoughts slithered in his mind on ways to make some easy money. He had already got away with a couple of goodies and now he would use the neighbourly approach. He was always sniffing the air for the knock of opportunity.

There was a knock at the door! Anne McCooey looked up from the partially clean floor and mentally cursed the disturbance. All her life she had been what people loosely call a 'clean-o-phoebe' and in the scheme of things this probably was one of the best phobias to have. She had a constant need to keep the world tidy. Whenever Jake took her for a walk around the lake, she always managed to collect a bag of rubbish. This was great for the environment and a fantastic way of keeping fit. Cleaning also kept Anne's mind busy when she was not at work. Lately the trouble with her mum and the grandkid issues had been quite a drain on her well-being. The weekend away at Nelson Bay was still on her mind, it had been a fun time. But now, the must do this and must get that list syndrome of shopping and housework was replacing the good memories. In truth to Anne, getting back to work was almost as much fun as holidays.

There was another knock.

'Hold your horses, I'm coming!' she yelled.

On seeing the old man at the door with a bemused look on his face, her first thought was caution, her second was that he was long over-due for a scrub. On opening the door and breathing in his unwashed odour and the stench of alcohol on his breath, she knew she was right on one count.

'Can I help you?'

'Morning ma'am, I'm your neighbour from up the street, name's Pat. Just thought I would pop in and welcome you to the area.'

Anne was on her guard, 'this poor urchin probably wants a handout,' she thought.

'Weather is pretty miserable,' he continued, seeking an invitation inside.

'I was just walking past; thought I'd ask you how your husband is doing? I heard about the incident at the lake on the grapevine.'

'Just a slight concussion and some bruises, he should be home soon,' she continued, now a little wary for her own safety.

'That's good,' he lied, 'I thought it sounded a lot more serious than that.'

Realising his welcome was on its last legs he asked,

'If I can be of any assistance don't hesitate to let me know? I walk past here quite often.'

Smiling, with his eternal cynicism burning bright, he took his leave.

'Anyhow Mrs I'll be off now.'

'Yes! I will tell my husband about your concern, thank you.'

Anne closed the door and took a deep breath.

'Thank god, I wonder what that old coot really wanted, maybe a second round of 'help yourself' to our things,' she thought.

When Jake got home from work Anne told him about the visit. He was not impressed. Later, that afternoon Anne was cooking dinner and saw Pat from the kitchen window, walking on the other side of the street heading north. Jake went out to have a word with him, but only caught up when Pat entered his house on the corner of Sorrell and Fennel Street. Unperturbed, Jake knocked on the door. It took a while but eventually the door opened. Jake tried not to show it, but for a moment he was in shock. Two dark eyes of the modern-day pirate Harvey cut him in half.

Harvey glared at him. 'Yeah, what do you want?'

There was a smart-ass air to this pip squeak of a man and Jake instantly disliked him. The feeling was mutual from Harvey's side as well, as he took a step closer. Jake stood his ground and verbally pounced,

'What I want is to know what your old man was doing at my place this morning?'

'He's not me old man, he's my uncle and how the hell would I know?'

'Try asking him.'

Just then the door opened wider, and Jake was hit with the stench of a dysfunctional house. Pat stood there with a smirk on his face,

'Just being neighbourly mate, you know, welcome to the area and such. I heard about your dust up down at the lake, thought to see if you are ok, that's all.'

'Who did you hear that from and since when is my health of any concern to you?'

'I heard a bloke talking about it down at the Royal and my concern stems from neighbourly instincts, I guess.'

Jake thought for a moment, 'Maybe Mick let slip, at his second watering hole the Royal, on both the lake incident and perhaps even the lotto win. Now this low life decided to case our place.'

'Well, my instinct tells me that there might be more to you than just neighbourly instincts, so in future keep clear of my house or I'll have you up for trespass!'

'And who the bloody hell do you think you are?' squealed Pat, feeling offended that this bloke read him like a book.

Harvey just stood there and glared at Jake, he had too much at stake to risk drawing police attention to his recent dealings but knew he would settle with this bloke in the future. As Jake turned to walk away, he sensed it coming and ducked a right hook from Pat. If it had connected it would have been a king hit. Jake turned and gave Pat a short sharp gut punch. Pat went down winded. Out of the corner of his eye Jake saw the pirate go for his leg strap. Harvey hesitated and thought twice about it, he then dragged his uncle inside and slammed the door.

Jake was shaken by the ordeal; he nearly pushed his luck a little too far. Both the pirate and the uncle had a look of embedded hate. As he headed home, he knew his first chore tomorrow would be to ring Moffitt.

CHAPTER 18

Wind

'The distinction between good and bad is a notional line
Scratched out in clean dirt with two
teams holding on to a rope,
One team called hate and the other team called hope.'

Moffitt was sitting in the office when Jake rang at 10am the next day. The humidity was as thick as carpet, the office ceiling fan and the lonely air conditioner were struggling to keep it in check. He thought an afternoon storm was set in concrete. The day's plan was to keep as cool as possible and to complete several reports before lunch. The afternoon's priority was an interview with Blaze Kennedy at Mary's Café and hopefully a trip to Cumberland Hospital to talk with Goliath Maitland and his Carer. He left off booking the latter just in case a cold beer was a better option on such a muggy day. Moffitt's hope was that this would all happen before mother-nature's anticipated fury.

'Hi Jake, how are you and how was the Nelson Bay trip?'

'Pretty good mate, we had a ball, it was only dampened by the break-in. I just rang to let you know about a little dust up I had yesterday with a nosey neighbour who gave Anne a bit of a fright. It turns out he lives with that Harvey Maitland character just up the road from my place.'

'Yeah, I know the joint Jake, its Harvey's Uncle's place. His name is Pat, and he is a real piece of work, must run in the family. What happened?'

Jake told Moffitt the facts of the incident in detail.

'If you want to take this further Jake, I must warn you, you followed him on to his property, so it would back-fire on you in court. I heard about the break in while you were away and of all the local crooks, that pair were a walk up start to be the offenders. But without evidence or a witness I would be pressed to get a warrant.'

'No, I gave him enough to stop his unwanted visits. I just wanted to keep you up to-date on local events. What is interesting was how this Pat knew about the little bump on the head I got from the lake incident, it was not exactly public knowledge. I suppose he could have overheard it at the pub?'

'I think you would be wise to stay clear of this lot Jake. They are well and truly on our radar now, but from the sound of it they will not forget your little visit in a hurry either. So, watch your back. I will send a team around to have a word to him about the trespass complaint, which might keep his head in his burrow for a while. By the way, after a couple of interviews this afternoon, I am going for a beer at the Rose, just the day for it, are you likely to be there'

'No mate, not tonight. Anne's home early she will most likely have plans.'

'No sweat we will catch up later and tell Anne not to worry about that bum Pat, this case is closing in like today's weather, I can feel it in the air.'

'Thanks Moffitt, keep your cool.'

'Yeah, that's my intention Jake.'

As the call ended Joan Debono walked in,

'I have some news on your mystery bloke at the fire boss.'

'What is it?'

'His name is Charlie Stark, a regular at the Rose and a mate of Jim Booth. Apparently, he is a writer and a bit of a snoop. He is always after new characters for a novel he is writing on the area. I've been told he is part of a local Italian family that lived in the Ellis Street property for over fifty years.'

'Stark doesn't sound Italian to me!'

'A name changes after his parents died, probably a pseudonym thing, you know writers.'

'Not really, but I will take that at face value and take him off my prime suspect list for now, thanks Bones. Do you want to come with me to interview this Blaze kid at the Lake Café?'

'Can I give that over-time a pass boss? I was planning a scuba dive with my boyfriend this afternoon, and you know, a cool off on the coast.'

'Yeah ok, hot day choices, enjoy the swim and watch out for sharks, I'll do my cooling off at the pub after the interview.'

'Thanks Moffitt, see you next Monday.'

'About Monday, take a uniform and put the wind up that Pat Maitland in Sorrel Street, it seems he may be up to his old tricks again. The old goat might be planning some more local robberies, and by the way, if he mentions a visit and punch that Jake laid on him, tread on his toes harder and tell him we are on to him. He will get the drift and hopefully move on and haunt another town.'

Mary was in a world of worry when Moffitt called into the café to have a talk with Blaze. There were no customers, most likely due to the heat and the pending storm. She was sitting there sipping on a coffee and staring at the lake with a distant look in her eyes. Moffitt surprised her.

'Hi Mary, is it warm enough for you?'

'Oh! Detective Moffitt, you startled me, yes, it is a scorcher.'

'Sorry I should have called first to let you know I was coming, but this heat has me all at sixes and sevens today. I was hoping to have a talk with a kid called Blaze Kennedy, I believe he works here.'

'Yes, he does and normally you would have caught him cleaning up the kitchen at this time of day, but it looks like he's gone walk-about again. I have not seen him since the bush fire weekend. I asked about him at the Lions Club soup kitchen on Saturday, but no one had seen him for a while. I had to employ another junior to cover for him. He is a troubled lad that Blaze and he has a history of doing this sort of thing. I was just sitting here thinking on whether I should give up on him and not give him another chance, when and if he returns. What did you want to talk to him about?'

'His name came up in some interviews I have conducted recently, and I wanted to cross check a few things.'

'Do you think he has been into some mischief?'

'Nothing concrete Mary, but I like to look under every rock. There is something going on around this lake and it is not all healthy activity. I just want to close this mystery for good and the clues are thin on the ground. I was going to do another interview today, but the weather wins this one, it's just too hot.'

'It must be, my brother Fritz just left here to go for a swim in the lake.'

'You wouldn't catch me in there ever, not after that eel sighting. I am one for seeing the bottom of things.'

'In more things than just water too, by the sound of it Mr Moffitt.'

'You're right there Mary. I will catch up with you later and have a coffee when the weather cools, give me a call if Blaze turns up?'

Charlie Stark like most writers loved to gather up his characters as a farmer gathers apples, with the hope of one day turning them loose as a good public yarn. His real name was Giovanni Starcelli, he chose to change it early in adult life. This came about due mainly to the 1950 Australian attitude to so called Wog's. Nationalities may change but the village mentality lingers. These days the children of those so-called Wog's call the new, 'New Australians' names and so it goes on ad infinitum.

Charlie, known by some as the whispering ghost, would stand still in the corner of the pub, looking into infinity. Some said he never wasted words on just chatter or jest. He spoke sparingly, like there were only so few words available to meet his needs. Charlie just stared, occasionally grinning or nodding an acknowledgement to a passing parade of multi-cultural characters. He was a thinking statue on the brink of an intelligent outburst that only infrequently occurred. His true thoughts centred on these characters, they could be simple, sad, good, or bad, or maybe a bit of each? In his list of stars there were players like Brian Magee, a lovely bloke, but not the sharpest tool in the shed. His pub nick name was 'Lantern' as in 'not too bright and had to be carried'. Another one of his pub favourites was the 'Blister', named by his work mates because the only time he appeared on the job was when the hard work was done. Such characters are with us every day, in every town, in every bar, beside the river and down quiet lanes. Some would be out of their depth in a parking lot puddle, others could swim across the Tasman Sea, being blessed with so much determination. Charlie, like nearly everyone else, had a backpack of prejudices for the road of life. Demographics change and colours blend, but most people have a back-pack weight that remains constant. There is good and bad in all of us and sometimes it is an easier walk down Harm Street than it is on Good Street. Hero's today is rare and generally a bit tattered. Fighting for what is right can be a lonely business, with very few rewards. But we do what we do to keep the wolf from the door.

Charlie stared into a picture on the pub wall, with an expressionless face. His thoughts were now adrift, and he followed the white rabbit down a well-known hole to escape the black dog that was always lurking:

'A 'fronte praecipitium a tergo lupi'. When you are caught between a rock and hard place, what else can you do?'

'From which end of the rope do we hang; the Loopy wolf fell for the trap that Stark had placed in its path. The snare triggered and the poor beast was air-born. Pent up tension within the bent sapling was now transferred onto the puzzled wolf. Flying high like a bird of prey above Stark's head, with the rope securely placed around old Loopy's neck, it floundered with all fours flapping like featherless wings. Then it thudded on the cliff face and hung there whimpering in pain. Goodness within Stark showered the injured wolf with empathy, and he hauled it to the safety of the cliff edge. Loopy bit his calf! Eventually the pain of their interlude faded, they became good friends and lived happily ever after as pet and master. Although both had limps, their attitudes were neither bad nor good, but somehow just balanced on the cliff edge of control.'

Charlie was always the protagonist in his thoughts.

Those thoughts floundered as Jim Booth said, 'g'day Chas,' a tag that Charlie detested but never challenged from this fellow. Of all his characters Jim was the closest thing to a mate, so he took the tag on the chin and ignored it.

'Good evening Jim.'

Jim, like Charlie, also sat on a cliff edge, caught between great thoughts and great sadness. This human affliction of depression was suffered in silence by many in today's world. Groups like 'Beyond Blue' had helped to bring the like poles together. Men like Jim and Charlie for the first time could begin to at least talk about it. Sitting in the corner of the pub having a quiet chat was all that was needed sometimes to help fine tune their lives when the precipice came into view.

Tonight, was different. The black dogs were now back in their kennels for both men. Jim was on a high with a pending nomination for town Mayor and Charlie had his characters poised for a grand finale. As with the tapestry of thoughts meandering through Charlie's head, real players in the surrounding world of minestrone cultures were gathering. These actors of life separated by only six degrees of knowing would soon find themselves and each other.

The final act was gathering in tandem with the eddy currents of high and low weather systems, with warm air to the north and a cold front to the south of the Sydney basin. Birds took to wing, dogs barked and even Elvis stirred.

CHAPTER 19

Storm

*'Between the towns of Self-doubt and Happiness, on the
Road of life, you will find tunnels and bridges.
The tunnels are where you confront your fears and the
Bridges are where you exploit your talents.'*

The carved effigy of a 'dreamtime' eel wrapped around the tongue of the Burramattagal cave like an ever-tightening tourniquet. From the time of the first stone chip, chiselled out by a stone-age man, and the following centuries of added work, combined with the effects of wind and rain erosion, the eel effigy had grown and filled with the detritus of age. A hot westerly breeze shuffled the leaves of nearby trees mimicking the spirits of Gilpani and a thousand other past survivors who had stood proud on the roof of their tribal rest to oversee their hunting grounds.

◆ ◆ ◆

In the wake of these Aboriginal warrior spirits, Fritz

finished a refreshing afternoon swim and came ashore on some low rocks adjacent to a protruding slab of sandstone. This large edifice jutted out like a giant dog's tongue lapping at the water. It was in an area where Hunts Creek met the open water of the lake. The lake walking trail was twenty or so metres to the north of this location and it was an unfamiliar place to Fritz. There was however something remarkably familiar on the only patch of sandstone that was not covered with leaves, moss, and bracken. It was the tag 'JOHN', neatly displayed in white paint. Fritz cursed the graffiti vandal, as he stood there drying off.

Mary was pretty upset that Blaze had let her down. Her thoughts were to get him back on track with a little love and attention. Obviously, he still had two sides to his nature, and it was an uphill battle to show him how far a little true respect could take him. It was a hot afternoon, and she was not normally one for walking, but recent events gave her a need to reflect a little. So, she decided to leave her car at the Cafe and take the scenic track around the lake to her home on North Rocks Road.

She left the Café in the capable hands of Aisha to cash up and to lock up for the day. Mary took the winding yellow path from the Café in front of the car park and headed towards the she-oak trail. There were two workers poisoning weeds and close by, children were feeding ducks in front of the caretaker's cottage. It was once home to the largest freshwater life-saving club in Australia. Further on an old drake called Gerry was wagging his tail for a feed. There were also a few swimmers back in the lake after a twenty-year absence, mainly due to water pollution. The car park was emptying out of day trippers, and a few remaining women and men were chatting in groups, while keeping an eye on their kids. On the other side of the car park Mary could see men liaising with women in parked cars, possibly not their wives. She thought for a moment about temptation, and its excuse, that being a lack of communication. In truth it had more to do with hormones and selfish gratification than the need for new love, but it was not her problem it was theirs.

Mary approached the fire trail where an Aboriginal bush tucker garden and a memorial to its creator stood as a reminder of the oldest inhabitants of this area. This helped to reinforce Mary's own belief that her ancestry and her willingness to help blend the surrounding cultures would one day be successful. A slight wind was blowing in the tops of the tall eucalypts and storm clouds were on the horizon as she approached the first bridge on the trail. She was still thinking about Blaze when she rounded a bend in the trail and saw Fritz's heavy frame between the gaps of several Iron Barks.

'Hi Fritz, how was the water?'

'Great Mary it was totally refreshing. What brings you out on a hot afternoon like this?'

'Oh, I left the car at the café and decided to walk home. I needed the exercise and some time to think.'

'What's the matter Sis? You know I'm a good listener.'

'It's Blaze Fritz. That policeman Mr Moffitt came to see him this afternoon and I had to tell him that I have not seen the boy for some time now. I feel he may be in some sort of trouble. On the other hand, if he returns, like he did last time, I don't know whether I should let him go or not.'

'That is the problem right there, you worry too much

about these street urchins. What they really need is a kick up the backside and a couple of years in the army. I have had my suspicions about that Blaze for some time now. He was somehow involved in the lighting of fires around here and see that graffiti over there on the rock, 'John' he calls himself, I would bet that he is responsible for that as well. It appeared around the same time he started at the Café.'

'Graffiti is a shout for recognition and a need to leave a legacy Fritz, just like Aboriginal cave art. I know some graffiti is unsightlier, but councils should encourage specific venues to capture this expression.'

'You always see purpose in madness Mary, this tagging crap is first class vandalism, we should be chopping off fingers for the privilege.'

'There you go again with that draconian streak embedded in you. Why don't you try to be more understanding Fritz? You know you get more bees with honey.'

'You also get more fly's Sis!'

'Anyhow, changing the subject, did you know that Blaze's grandmother was half aboriginal, like me?'

'How would I know that? He is as white as chalk and besides, it doesn't matter, these young drop kicks are part of the same broken broom problem, sharing in the spoils and sweeping up the handouts until they take off on another adventure.'

'You're wrong Fritz. The problem is that the spirits of some of these lost souls live in a fractured nightmare with no direction. They flicker backwards and forwards from a 'Dreamtime' of perceived peace to the modern reality of 'Struggle Street'. Because most people are like you and carry their intolerance and prejudices for life, a lot of these sad cases seek like peers. Then live up to intolerant expectations and disappear. 'Walk-about' is not just a concentration problem, I think their spirit wanders off looking for some peace in nature and their physical form follows along for the ride. The ones that drink and lose control are just frightened to face the demons and try to dull their minds. This then becomes a permanent habit and the rot sets in.

'Well Mary, I know you mean well but I think most live on 'Struggle Street' because of laziness and our government's handout mentality.'

Mary was starting to get on the soap box a little and her relaxed state was under attack. Fritz always had a way of charging her emotions and in the process, help answer problems. Although they were worlds apart in the way they thought, Mary needed Fritz to keep her perspective balanced.

'No Fritz, you can't see the big picture. You think the indigenous problem is just a small part of our modern society. The active lobby groups, stolen generation and a few 'Mabo' lawyers are just the tip of the iceberg. There are hidden multitudes of mixed genes out there. The wander lust of a lot of the new age Australian traveller has its roots in a 'Dreamtime' past. The skeletons in closets of our history covered up a lot of the 'out of wedlock' baby boom that occurred from the time the 'First Fleet' arrived. Do the math, boat loads of horny white boys and a few girls, add into the mix aboriginal girls free for the taking and what have you got. That is right, there are actually a lot of unknown success stories out there and that's why I feel the need to help Blaze.'

Mary had her answer and Fritz just shuffled his feet and gave up. In the process he uncovered a strange shape in the rock. He dug at it with his foot and scraped out the dirt and leaf matter until it disappeared under some bracken fern. In the other direction it meandered across the surface of the rock slab like the body of a snake or an eel. Then it disappeared over the edge between the roots of a Banksia tree.

'What do you think this is Mary?'

'It looks old, I think it's a carving. I knew I felt something here Fritz, this place has a strange calling to it. I think we may have discovered an Aboriginal ceremonial site. I know a lot of people who will be extremely interested to explore it further.'

'Come on Fritz, it's too hot here and its getting dark, walk me home and I will shout you a drink.'

'Sounds ok to me Mary, you don't have to ask twice.'

A yellow Lamborghini pulled up on the access road between the lake and North Rocks Road, as Mary and Fritz made their way to Mary's house. They could make out the well-built driver, but the passengers were not visible through the dark shaded windows. The car stood out like 'Where's Wally' in a sea of people. Fritz thought it strange and just glanced at the driver, who offered a sneer in return for his unwanted interest. The occupants stayed in the car until Mary and Fritz were out of site. As Rick got out of the car, he issued a dog command to Dmitry,

'Stay put and phone if there are any snoops.'

From the access road it was only a short walk, so he

headed off down the trail to the cave. He had only been here once before, the night that nosey camper got knocked out, when he had told Harvey to shut up shop. This second visit was an annoyance he did not need. Harvey was turning out to be more trouble than his worth.

Dmitry Ibrovski had spent most of his adult life as a paid hitman. He had a background of crime that found its roots in the Russian Mafia in the madness that followed the fall of the Soviet State and the Berlin Wall. A misunderstanding with his boss, a powerful and wealthy oligarch, over a transaction that went bad, caused the tide to turn on Dmitry. There was a sudden need to flee Russia. He had been surviving for two years when he met Rikos Hassan in Beirut. They were like poles of hate but found a common goal in villainy. The offer of work in Australia was too good to reject. With false passport in hand, Dmitry arrived in Sydney on a separate flight to Rikos. He had scored himself a permanent driver-enforcer role in crime, not your usual undocumented immigrant. He was a Mastiff hound on a chain with a detached indifference. His one pleasure in life was blues music, so he now sat back and rested in the Lamborghini listening to the soft, dulcet tones of 'Georgia on my mind'. His true thoughts were nowhere special.

The night air was slightly cooler, but it was still sticky and uncomfortable. The storm continued to build. From the veranda where Jake and Anne now sat, they could see two thunder heads, one to the south-west and one to the north-west. They stood like two giant mushroom mountains with the eerie glow of an orange sunset bridge joining them together. Stars came out and the fruit-bats from the trees by the river near the Female Factory began their nightly migration to orchards and gardens on the Hornsby Plateau. Anne had no plans for the night and neither of them felt sleepy, but the nature enthusiast in Jake had a thought.

'How about we go spotlighting on the lake reserve fire trail?'

'What about that storm?'

'It's hours off and on a night like this the sugar gliders may be active, it's been years since I have seen any down there and besides a walk through the bush at night will be fun, especially with you'

'You are persuasive. I suppose it's a primal thing, yeah why not.'

Fifteen minutes later they entered the Reserve, the Café was locked up and there was a light on in Fritz's cottage. Both his and Mary's cars were out the front. They decided not to disturb them and walked on past. An oily grease smell from an old auto wreck that had been recently removed from the scrub, greeted their nostrils as they walked from the parking area. Further along the trail there was a whiff of fox urine, despite the baiting program they were always around. But apart from the unwanted ferals and old rusting junk from the modern world, the forest was alive with native animal life. Cockatoos and galahs were bedding in for the night high in the trees and Anne's torch light caught a large goanna heading home. They were a kilometre down the trail when with luck Jake's torch highlighted a movement on the road just metres in front. It was a five-foot red bellied black snake enjoying the extended heat from the day. It was still quite active and took off in a slow slide of defiance, thankfully in the opposite direction.

There is a feeling you get at times when you are totally relaxed. It runs in the opposite direction to common sense; it is a sudden awareness. It might be an urge to ring home or a feeling the phone is going to ring seconds before it does. Call it spiritual or a sixth sense, call it what you like, but it exists. Jake felt it now. He was blocking the anxiety it was generating, somewhere deep in his subconscious mind, by maintaining the excitement of discovery. He and Anne walked on, spot lighting the trees in search of the elusive sugar gliders.

'Up there Anne!' Jake whispered. He was pointing the torch light at a movement on the branch tip of a large Ghost Gum.

'I see it!' she responded with delight, as the sugar glider took to the air and drifted gently to a neighbouring tree trunk. Jake's heart skipped a beat of love from the excitement on her face.

'That was just magical Jake.'

Jake's attention was suddenly diverted to the other side of the creek. He stared with that searching look, both seeing and thinking at the same time. Anne, still with excitement in her thoughts saw his distraction.

'What's caught your eye now my love?'

'Did you see that? I just saw a flash from a torch light over near that bend in the creek.'

'So what? We're out tonight and others also walk here Jake.'

'Yes, but that light came from an area off the track and roughly where I got clobbered the other week. The mystery attacker might be back.'

'And what is the brave Jake going to do, bail him up and make a citizen's arrest. Don't even think it, that storm is brewing up fast and we should get home before it hits.'

'We have plenty of time to finish the circuit now Anne, the crossing is just up ahead we will be home in an hour. Come on babe, I promise we will not leave the trail. We will quietly walk past the spot and just listen. If we see anything suspicious, we jog home and let the police know.'

'I don't know Jake, it's a bit scary. No stopping, straight home, that's it, ok?'

'Ok by me Watson let's get going.'

'Lead on Sherlock!'

Fifteen minutes later they were close to the site where Jake saw the light.

'That's the camp site over there.' He whispered as he pointed. 'And that rocky spot near that big gum tree is where I took the blow.'

'Come on Jake there is no one around. Let's get out of here, it's creepy.'

Just as they were about to walk off there was another flash of light. It seemed to become up from the ground adjacent to a big boulder and some scrub. Jake edged a little closer while Anne stood her ground now scared and annoyed.

'Look Anne, there is someone down at the lake, they are in some sort of cave right on the water's edge.'

'Jake! It's time to go...'

Anne's unfinished response startled Jake, he spun

around to see his wife gagged with the large hand of a dark silhouette, but all he could focus on was the gun on Anne's temple. His stomach turned with fear, and he broke out in a cold sweat. The wind picked up a little, it was hot and prickly and a voice with a mid-east accent told Jake to get on his knees. Anne was visibly shaking now, and Jake's sense of helplessness reached a peak.

'Put that bag over your nosey head and do it up tight or both of you will be feeding maggots in the morning.'

It was a grizzled accent and slightly muffled, but it had conviction. Jake saw the white money bag on the ground in front of his knees and did what he was told. His thoughts were scattered. He had anger at his own stupidity and a rising fear for Anne's wellbeing. But above his anguish he also realised that not seeing the strangers face may give them a chance of living through this ordeal. Rick put a bag into Anne's hand and told her to put it on. He then pushed her towards Jake and told Jake to get up. With the gun now shoved in Jake's back he marched them down to the cave.

Harvey was doing an evening pickup for a deal in the morning when Rick rang. Rick was not happy when Harvey said he was at the cave. Initially he was not overly concerned when he was told about the cave warehouse but recent attention to the area had changed his attitude. At their last meeting Harvey was told to wrap it up and find a garage somewhere. The attachment to his boyhood adventures and his lazy streak added to the thought that there was no rush. When a bloke like Rick says jump and there is no action you can become an underworld statistic

over night

Harvey was packing it and not just the drugs. He heard a noise outside the cave and doused the light. At that moment, the outside world lit up like Luna Park as a bolt of lightning struck.

Two billowing giant ebony green storm fronts were now rubbing shoulders to the west of Parramatta. For the last two hours they had been in a Mexican stand-off, neither giving way, and as the pressures and electrical charges built, the relief valve finally blew with the force of a hurricane that cut a swathe from Westmead to Hornsby. This axe of power dissected the Lake Reserve up-rooting trees and stamping the locals with the fear of nature's fury. An associated lightning strike at the 'Female Factory' tore the heart out of a giant grapefruit tree but failed to wake a nearby slumbering giant who was dreaming of pirates, caves, and unknown faces.

At first it was just the feel of a hot wind buffeting the bag over Jake's head, but then the lightning struck so close that its pressure wave knocked both he and Anne on to their knees. As a boulder was pushed aside, Harvey peered out to an angry world, an angry man and a couple of people on their knees with bags over their heads.

'Drag 'em inside knuckle-head before we all get killed!'

Harvey heard the anger in Rick's voice. He shuffled the newcomers into his lair and made them sit at the back of the cave next to the recently packed boxes of drugs and stolen items. Golf ball size hail, travelling nearly parallel to the ground, were being forced along by a two hundred kilometre an hour cyclonic wind. They were bouncing off the rocks like bullets in a war zone. Rick crawled inside the cave, all the time with gun in hand and pointed at Anne.

'Seal the bloody cave, idiot!' He screamed at Harvey.

With the cave entry secure he turned to see Rick screwing a silencer on the gun, water was dripping off his greasy ponytail and he was staring at Harvey with cold black eyes. Harvey did not know what to say, in the end he thought to break the tension in Rick with some humour.

'If I knew you were going to bring guests, I would have done a shop boss.'

'Just shut your smart mouth and tape up theirs, as well as their hands. You pair turn around or the lady gets damaged!'

Knowing he had no choice Jake turned and told Anne to do the same, she was starting to sob.

He tried to comfort her by saying, 'it will be ok baby, just do what they say.'

He also sensed the enclosed surroundings, and his old fear came back to run in parallel with the current nightmare. He instinctively knew that not seeing a face was to their advantage, but Jake had heard this second bloke's voice before, and it was recently familiar. Then the penny dropped.

'It was the pirate with attitude, Maitland.'

That meant that the other bloke could be Rikos from the racetrack. Jake's anxiety now grew with realisation that his knowledge of this pair could prove fatal if Harvey saw his face.

Rick rang up Dmitry on the mobile and Jake and Anne listened to every word.

'Privyet, Dmitry speaking.'

'English fool English! Sit tight until the storm passes then come down the trail to the lake.'

'Sorry comrade, how will Dmitry find you?'

'Give me a call when you get to the lake's edge, I will find you, I will need a hand with some boxes.'

Harvey taped both sets of hands securely. Anne was struggling when he wrapped duct tape around her mouth. Jake felt her fear and responded.

'Hurt her and I'll bloody kill ya, you prick!' he yelled.

A fist crossed his jaw as payment for the outburst and as Harvey taped his legs and then his mouth, he kicked out with all his fury. The captives then just sat there in fear and temper, pondering their fate. When Harvey finished with his guests, he said nothing to Rick, but he had recognised Jake's voice and knew that this pair would not be leaving the cave alive. Rick told him to get off the rock shelf and sit on the sand, at the water's edge. He was now starting to fear for his own life, the nervous facial tick had come back and was running at full speed. His hands were spread out supporting his weight and small waves of water were lapping at his fingers, indicating that the outside turmoil had found it is way to the inside drama. Not another word was said.

Elvis was laying half curled in his pre-hibernation pose wrapped around the canvas bundle of rotting flesh, sensing the vibrations of man-made and natural storms. He rested there unmoved, barely two metres from fingers wriggling in his water world.

Long ago another storm had raged beyond the safety of this cave. It was a storm of fire not water, but it also generated apocalyptic fear within the hearts and minds of some of the inhabitants. Gilpani, Pinacan and other younger minds had sat in silence as an Elder calmed their fears with stories of the Dreamtime past.

There was no calming the fears washing through the thoughts of Jake and Anne. The intent and silence of their captors was in itself a panic invoking struggle. Outside the storm raged on. Trees could be heard cracking and tumbling, even over the cacophony of wind and hail. The wind was talking in whispers and screams through the fissures and cracks within their prison. Anne was resting her head on Jake's lap; he could offer no other comfort. Harvey's frustration was growing, and Rick just sat there in silence. He looked around the cave at the resplendent Aboriginal art and was unmoved. His mind was racing with outcomes and survival thoughts. The basics of a murderous plan were hatched, this unknown cave made for an excellent tomb. All that was required now was a phone call and a let up in the harsh weather.

The cave was still quite warm from the day's extreme heat. Harvey sat with sweat beads running down his temples. He splashed his face with water and noticed a movement in the shadows where the cave tongue kissed the sand. His facial expression froze with fear as an old nemesis had come back to haunt him. A large red belly black snake was still active from the day's heat, and it slithered along the shoreline in his direction.

'Don't move!' Rick commanded, as he took aim. The first shot thudded in the sand, he missed, and the snake took off at a lightning pace across Harvey's outstretched legs, its fangs scratching his arm in the process... The second shot popped Harvey's knee cap off like a cork as he tried to dive clear of the snake. The snake disappeared and left Harvey writhing in agony and screaming with pain. Blood leached through the sand and into the lake. Elvis began to stir, his senses now stimulated with a familiar taste. Rick's empathy was non-existent as he told Harvey to shut up. Harvey's next shock came when Rick started to duck-tape his hands and mouth. His last audible expression was, 'What the f...!' The only smile left on his face now was a crescent moon birth mark.

Nature is cruel when it comes to survival, human nature can complement its extremes. Harvey's life of cruelty was flashing through his mind. He was incapable of understanding this new situation. Laying there in pain with flashes of Blaze and Golly playing in a fractured movie, with his Mum and of all people his sister Sally as extras.

The spiritual peace of the ancients was now shattered. The ancestors from the cave's long and mystic history chanted through the winds of nature for retribution. The response came quick.

Atrax Robustus was not another tough criminal drug

lord, but he and his female were the Bonny and Clyde of one spot in the cave wall. Sydney funnel web spiders have virulent venom and even though humans are not their intended prey it can kill them quicker than any other mammal. Tingling around the mouth, muscle twitching and salivation start the process, hypertension and death ends it.

Rick moved back to his spot on the rock shelf now happy with his decision on the way ahead. Harvey could die in pain and the love birds could slowly fade into oblivion in their own time. He rested his head on the inner side wall of the cave, not far from the teeth of the eel effigy, and closed his eyes for a moment. The gale had eased, the phone rang and a spider bit.

Harvey was lying on the beach making muffled noises of pain when Rick pushed the entry rock aside. A cool breeze flooded the cave, and all was quiet until Rick called out to Dmitry. Nature's devastation on the outside was more than obvious, even within the focused thoughts of Rick. There were streams of water flowing into the gaping holes where tree roots once clung and all around a weakened structure of the forest had broken limbs still falling.

Dmitry heard Rick's angry call and found the track to the cave through all the broken vegetation.

'Crawl in there and drag those two boxes of drugs out, we will be leaving that dip-shit Harvey to rot in his cave with his guests.'

Rick was starting to feel ill and had a tingling sensation around his mouth.

'Are you ok boss, you don't look the best?'

'A stinking spider bit me! We have to get out of here

quick and get to a hospital.'

Dmitry shoved Jake and Anne aside without saying a word and dragged the boxes out. This gave them a little more room at the rear of the cave. Jake had felt around during the night and found a sharp piece of stone. He had made some progress on removing the taping around his hands, so he still had hope of escape. His love for Anne and her safety were calming weapons against his fear. As the entry rock was pushed back into place all was quiet again and hope faded a little.

The big Russian carried both boxes with ease and followed a now staggering Rick along the broken track back to the car. In an area where nearly every tree had come down, a broken limb weighing close to a ton hung precariously by a piece of bark to a ghost gum. The giant tree had withstood the onslaught and its branch as if by design hovered in wait. It fell in silence and in a blink, Dmitry was back with his family in Russia for a fleeting moment, until darkness won.

Rick, now skewed to the earth, had new pain to contemplate and if he survived perhaps a new fear arachnophobia.

CHAPTER 20

Tempest

Clear water ran over lichen covered rocks making creeks sing with quenching joy. The rain had stopped, and the lake water quivered in the aftermath. Olive green leaves freckled with suspended water droplets glistened from the soft morning light that peeked from a blue-sky gap between cloud and horizon. All was still but for croaking frogs bedazzled by the sudden change from dry heat to moist coolness. Finches flitted, worms wriggled, and the forest floor moved with creatures. New homes had been created and old homes destroyed by falling trees and branches, but the forest seemed to have a new lease of life. In the distance there were other noises, men talking, people running, chainsaw stop-starting and a woman's fearful scream.

Bob Stickles got an early morning call about the damage caused by the storm. His SES group had been sent to various locations in the storm affected area. He wisely left calling Steve and Mick to last, knowing full well that yesterday's heat would have meant a late-night session of drinking at the pub.

Steve was in the shower when the phone rang, he knew it was Saturday because Cheryl left the cleaning products out. He was not yet accustomed to this new weekly ritual, mainly because it was making his life shorter. It seemed like it was only yesterday that he was scrubbing this same shower screen. It was always a puzzle why some women could not wait till something was dirty before cleaning it. Still, he would not complain it was all part of getting to know each other. The idea to move in together was a joint decision, both had lived alone for some time and adjustments were going to be needed from both sides. As he took the call from Bob, he was reminded by Cheryl that breakfast was ready. Having the morning bacon and eggs cooked for you was part of the adjustments that almost made cleaning the shower screen fair.

'Good morning Bob, what's up? 'Hi Steve, the big blow last night caused quite a bit of damage. I have most of the crews out cutting trees and clearing roads, I need you and Mick to check out Mary's Café at the Lake, the area copped a hammering.'

'Right on it mate, is Mick expecting me?'

'Yeah, he is, by the way could you drive past Jake's place and let him know the Energy Matters control room has been trying to reach him all night. They have about 40,000 customers off. I was just talking to his mate Sully about some power line problems, and he said he is not answering the home phone or the mobile. They even tried Anne's mobile'

'Ok mate I will, but that's strange I walked past last night and both cars were parked in the yard.'

'Give us a call if you find him. I must go the calls are backing up, bye for now.'

Half an hour later Steve rang back, there was no one home at Jake's place, but the cars were still there.

Goliath awoke early to an eerie still and a strange scent in the air. It was the sweet smell of cut timber. He had slept through the storm and was well rested but strangely unhappy. Carnation cottage suddenly appeared to be a cold and uncomfortable place. This mood swing was not something Golly had knowledge of it was more to do with the way his brain was reacting to his recent decision to avoid medication. For once breakfast was not his first thought, the urge to be near his tree of strength had a stronger pull. Still dressed in his flannel pyjamas he opened the rear door and stepped past the crumpling convict wall. At first, he stood there paralysed, not knowing why his tree of growth had turned into two. Suddenly he felt its pain and frustrations flowed like a fire storm, as the canyons of anguish creased his brow. The lightning strike had cut it down the middle like a split log. It was weeping the orbs of its golden fruit and scattered them like teardrops on the verdant green lawn. Golly's tears flowed in unison with his dying friend as a volcano of angry pain erupted in his mind. He gathered up the tears of fruit in a plastic fertilizer bag and ran and ran, hoping to leave the pain behind.

Ten minutes later the 000 emergency switchboards were being flooded with calls from Fleet and Factory streets North Parramatta. A man wearing pyjamas had gone berserk, he was running and throwing grapefruit at people and houses. He was last seen in Bourke Street heading towards Lake Parramatta Reserve, after shoving a Mr Simpson through the window of the liquor shop. Ambulance and Police radio calls went out for units to attend.

Molly Moffitt rolled over and nudged Harry from his snoring slumber.

'Sorry dear but I have a 7.00 am flight to catch.'

It took Moffitt a few minutes to get motivated but within the hour they were walking out the front door showered and with a belly full of cereal. The storm had left a few branches on the driveway, but they were quickly cleared, and the happy couple were on their way. Molly visited her mother in Perth at least once a year, the added benefit for Moffitt was that it offered a welcome short break from married life. The short-lived bachelor experience was great for a while, but in the end, it just reinforced the reason he got married again. This was made obvious by the accumulating dirty dishes and the pile of dirty clothes that appeared in the house over the two weeks that Molly was gone.

The ever-growing traffic problems on the M4 and M5 diminished his enjoyment of a Saturday morning drive, so he decided to take the Harbour Bridge route home. This was a longer and more expensive journey but overall, it was a safer and less stressful drive. Moffitt had heard on the news about the damage the storm had caused and was going to head into the office to see if he could be of help. He also heard a call on the police radio and three words got his attention, Lake Parramatta, grapefruit, and pyjamas. As Moffitt exited the Epping tunnel his phone rang.

Bones was called in for a Saturday shift due to the storm damage and was keen to bring him up to speed on the latest lake drama.

'Morning Moffitt, we have had a bit of trouble down at the lake. Goliath Maitland from the Cumberland facility is on a rampage through North Parramatta, the last report had him smashing an SES worker with a bag of fruit and running off down the trail on the north side of the dam. What's your location?'

'Epping tunnel, I just heard the radio call, look I'll come in on foot from the North Rocks Roadside, with luck I should be there in about ten minutes. You follow him on foot, take a Taser, don't take him alone, and wait for me ok.'

'Ok boss.'

Moffitt pulled up behind a yellow Lamborghini now peppered with dimples from the hailstorm. At first, he was puzzled by the site of an expensive wreck, but as he headed down the track towards the lake the story became clearer. He had seen some strange things in his career, but what captured his vision now topped the list. Fifty metres down the trail a dozen large trees had fallen over all in the same direction, in an area the size of a quarter acre block. It was like a strike in a ten-pin bowling centre. On the edge of this carnage next to a giant tree was Fritz carrying she-oak branch towards two strangers crushed under a large tree limb. The other surprising features were two crushed boxes and a covering of white powder on the surrounding ground.

'Morning Fritz what's the go here then? It looks like you have made a real drug bust!'

Fritz let the comment slip, he had placed two rocks adjacent the branch one for a fulcrum and one for a chock.

'Great timing Detective, I will lever the log up if you could slip that rock under the branch, we might make life a little more comfortable for at least one of these blokes.'

Moffitt was impressed at how cool Fritz was with the situation. He was also amazed at his strength. He shuffled the rock in place while Fritz held the weight, despite the lever it was still quite a feat.

'This bloke is dead, that one is near enough but going through weird spasms. He is twitching and frothing at the mouth like his got rabies, mumbled something about a spider bite. I've called for an Ambulance.'

'I know him.' Moffitt responded, 'His name is Rikos Hassan. He would be the owner of the Lamborghini.'

'Yeah, the other bloke must be his driver. They were here last night, looked pretty suspicious too, and I was going to call you this morning.'

'I'll get the details later Fritz, could you call the police as well and get a back-up vehicle down here. All mayhems broken loose this morning, I have a mental patient heading this way along the lake path, I have to go, we will talk later.'

Moffitt headed off at a jog straight down the track to the lake. His mind was now racing with detective scrutiny, cases of drugs, Harvey and Rikos, and then Jake's knock on the head. It all came together at once and added up to a storehouse. The penny then dropped.

'There must be a cave around here somewhere?' He thought.

Steve was clearing branches from the road in front of the Café and talking to Mary about the storm when Golly came running down the hill. Mick had the chainsaw halfway through a grey gum as the big bloke came through the tunnel and into the reserve. He swung the bag of grapefruit so hard that Mick was airborne for a metre and laid spread eagled and winded on the road. It was lucky the chainsaw jammed in the log. Both Mary and Steve ran to assist. Golly did not even stop, he just kept on running down the path to the dam wall.

Billy Chan had left home early for a look at the storm damage. There were trees down everywhere on the north bank of Hunts Creek, so he headed from his reserve entry point near the rear of Kings School and followed the fire trail and south bank track. Bill was in a good mood despite the awful damage to the reserve. Susan had returned home during the night. After a long talk they resolved a lot of issues and it seemed like their marriage was worth saving. Billy was just about at the Café when he saw Mary standing by an SES man laid out on the road. That is when he heard the scream. Mrs Barker and her dog Milo had just gone for an unrequested swim.

Golly had shoved her out of the way and booted poor Milo like a football. Mrs Barker was barely able to stay afloat when Steve dived in and saved her, she was pretty shaken up. Seconds later Billy was in the water too, poor Milo looked dead but a minute after he bought the dog to shore it came around. Although bruised and battered Milo would live. They were now concerned about Mrs Barker; she was in serious shock.

Steve and Billy helped take all the war wounded including Mick over to the Café so Mary could tend their
wounds. Steve was on the phone to get an Ambulance for
Mrs Barker when a police car pulled up, it was Joanne De-
Bono, Moffitt's offsider. She ran off in hot pursuit of Golly
and five minutes later Steve and Bill followed. The day
was just starting to warm up in more ways than one.

A scream faded in the background and the ground near
the Burramattagal cave rumbled, as two bulls of men
raged from opposite direction to the inevitable clash between good and evil.

Golly had slowed to a walking pace but was still agitated.
He was talking to himself when Bones came up behind
him, she had done what Moffitt had asked and kept her
distance. The Taser was in her right hand and fully
charged. As Golly approached the pirate cave of his youth,
he was hoping to find Harvey, the only person he thought
could help him with the pain he was experiencing. He
dropped his bag of fruit and a couple of grapefruit tears
rolled down the hill onto the cave rock and dropped into
the now still lake water. As he watches them sink the feeling of loss returned as did his anger. He turned and saw
Bones watching him from behind a tree. She was caught
off guard for a second when he launched at her with all
his rage. The Taser fired and hit his leg. Golly stumbled
for a second, but the giant man seemed unaffected. He
reached out with two powerful hands, but Bones fended
him off and ran down towards the cave.

Moffitt was a ball of sweat as he jumped over the last
fallen tree on the trail. He saw Golly running towards

Bones and he crash tackled the giant with all the skills left over from his Rugby days. They rolled like a bulldozer onto the roof of the cave. The spirits of the past made way and the carved eel effigy groaned in one last sacrificial crossing ceremony, this time by two modern day warriors. The rock tongue collapsed like a trapdoor and pivoted on the cave's inner shelf as the two giants followed the grapefruit into the lake.

Harvey heard the commotion outside and as the roof fell, he launched himself to a protected area to the right. His pain trebled as the slab of rock crushed his lower torso. His upper body floated up and down as he gasped for air at every opportunity in the small niche between rock and water. Reaching with his taped hands for body support, he managed to find it on the canvas wrapped remains of Blaze Kennedy.

Elvis stirred from his muddy cocoon at the influx of new blood and slowly his pectoral fins propelled him to a new neck to feast on. Harvey's trauma diminished with every nibble that Elvis took until his last gasp of air. His last thought was of Marvin and the way he died. When he saw him sitting on the dam wall that night, he could not resist the urge to throw one of Golly's grapefruit at a hated target and so in the end Marvin too got his retribution and Harvey got his justice.

Jake and Anne were sitting with their thoughts when the external noise of people dissolved their fears and again gave them new hope. As the cave roof came down with a frightening thud the inner shelf protected them from a crushing death. Jake was now frantically wearing away at his bindings as his thought of rescue heightened.

All the fight had left Golly when he hit the water. Unable

to swim he floundered for a few minutes until Moffitt managed to save him. Steve and Bill showed up in time to drag the big man ashore where Bones was happy to get some cuffs on him. Moffitt finally smiled.

'Great work team looks like this lake caper has yielded some answers at last. It's a drug stash and my guess are that this cave is full of secrets. Steve could you and Bob pull that rock aside and Bones could you go up to my car and get a torch.'

Jake finally cut through the hand taping and removed his mouth gag just as the boys moved the rock aside. The entrance was considerably smaller, and the boys fell over in shock as a hand came out and familiar voice shouted,

'Get us out of here!'

The whole group were stunned! Moffitt ran to the cave entrance to assist.

'What the hell are you doing in there Jake McCooey?'

'Well, I'm not having a lakeside picnic that's for sure Moffitt and Anne's with me, we are a little worse for wear.'

'We will have you out in a jiff mate just hang in there!' Steve screamed, as he and Bill dug frantically around the entry.

'Moffitt?'

'I'm here Jake.'

'You will need a rescue unit in here, that weasel Harvey Maitland has been shot and when the roof collapsed, I heard him gurgling on the water's edge.'

'Ok Jake, right on it.'

Moffitt called for an Ambulance, a rescue unit and some back up, he then directed them to come in via the short route off North Rocks Road.

Jake took the bindings off Anne and she fell into his arms sobbing. He kissed her gently on the lips and said he was sorry. The guilt he was feeling for their predicament overwhelmed all his fears and the relief of pending rescue caused tears to well in his eyes. Anne felt his warmth as tears on their cheeks mingled, she kissed him back and whispered softly in his ear,

'I love you Jake McCooey you are my hero, but next time I say let's go home I mean it!'

Jake assisted Anne through the cave entrance and the boys reached in to help. Five minutes later they were free and there were hugs all round. The adventure unfolded into reunited happiness, with stories to last.

They all stood around like soldiers after a battle. Bones and Fritz came back with a torch, blankets, and an army of uniformed saviours. Fritz also had news that Rikos had died on the way to hospital. Apparently, he was mumbling something about Harvey, the hate talk was mixed with fading expletives on spiders and storms. Bones and the Ambulance Officers wrapped blankets around Jake and Anne, who were still suffering from a little shock.

Bill was standing guard over Golly who was securely handcuffed to a fallen Ironbark tree. The big bloke looked up at Bill like it was all one big adventure and smiled,

'Are we going to do some fish'n here Bill?'

'No mate the big fellow has been caught, so I guess there won't be any more fishing for a while.'

'That's ok Bill I'll see you at next week's sausage sizzle.'

Bill looked at Golly with sadness and wondered at this normally gentle giant's ability to switch between worlds of carnage and calm. The best days were now behind Golly, there would be no more bush walks or sausage sizzles, but perhaps his grapefruit tree would sprout in the new seasons ahead.

Moffitt sensed justice may have been achieved without a drawn-out court battle and highly payed defence barristers, the sort that men like Rikos had direct access to. His attention now focussed on Harvey Maitland and Blaze Kennedy.

Steve was first to notice the stranger, he turned to tell Moffitt and as he pointed all heads followed. There on the hill, amongst fallen trees and debris, stood the pasty face and ubiquitous Mr Stark, like the 'Statue of Rhodes' welcoming home his warriors, he smiled at last he had found his heroes.

CHAPTER 21

Calm

Moffitt gazed from the Café balcony with awe at the destruction. It was only now after all the dust of the drama had settled that he could focus on the power of nature. The bared limbs of the ravaged trees were like arms reaching skyward screaming for help. Tears welled in Mary's eyes when he told her of the discovery of Blaze Kennedy's body. He also mentioned the interview with Goliath Maitland which sadly revealed his involvement in the murder. As for the outcome of the trial it was a forgone conclusion that Goliath would be transferred to a more secure mental institution. He decided to deliver the news directly to Mary before she read it in the press. While he was there, he also invited her and Fritz to the community de-briefing session that was being arranged.

It was a Friday afternoon two weeks before Christmas and the lake incident community de-brief was to be held in the beer garden of the Rose and Thorn Hotel. Police Public Relations came up with the idea and the event was by invitation only. It included representatives of all the players in the incident from Bob Stickles of the SES to Jake's mate Sully from Energy Matters and all the locals who were friends of Marvin. A reporter from the Advisor Newspaper was invited, as were representatives from the Environmental Protection Agency, the Police Rescue Unit, and the Fire Brigade. Jim Booth and Fritz were the Local Council reps, other's included the Aboriginal Land Council rep Dan French, who was the pub patron they called Ice. Even Charlie Stark got an invite due to his interest in the total affair. Jake had begun to warm to this bloke a little. Jim Booth had told him about Stark's depression problems and the empathy he shared silently with the locals.

Paul from the Rose and Thorn had closed off the beer garden to the general public and offered a good discount on the afternoon's finger food. Everyone turned up anxious to hear the outcome of the Coroner and the forensic report on Harvey. At this stage, only a few were aware of the other body that was found or the eel's involvement.

Moffitt took the microphone and pointed out that the meeting was more than an information session. It was also to convey a big thank you to the people involved in the storm clean up and for their help in a complex situation involving human and natural dangers. He went on to point out that the lake reserve was still a mess and for the time being the only part of the reserve open to the public was Mary's Café. Moffitt looked around the room with his focused police eyes and when the group was silent, he continued.

'At first the police divers were unable to retrieve the body that was wedged under the fallen section of the cave. A crane was required to lift the fallen slab of sandstone.

The area that this cave incident occurred in took the brunt of the storm damage and an access road had to be built to allow access for the crane. This took three days to build from the North Rocks Road entry point. Also, upon discovery of the Aboriginal artwork, the local land council and the EPA insisted all care be taken to preserve the site. Once the crane was in position it gently raised the sandstone slab using the rock shelf as a pivot point. When it was back to its original height above the water two large boulders were placed in position to support the weight. This would allow future study of the Aboriginal drawings. The police divers were sent to retrieve the body of Harvey Maitland and discovered another body at the same location. DNA identification was required on the latter due to decomposition and missing body parts, it was found to be that of Blaze Kennedy. He was a former employee of Mary's Café and had been reported missing a month earlier.'

After his explanation of the discovery of two bodies and the effort in their retrieval the crowd went quiet. With that the Advisor reporter jumped in and asked the first question.

'Did you say body parts missing, was the Eel involved?'

'I thought that would get a bite, but before you go running off with more killer EEL madness, let me continue. Yes, there were signs of carrion interference on both bodies. Maitland's had been mauled and the canvas wrap around Kennedy had been chewed through to allow access to the body, but none of this caused the death of either person. In the case of Blaze Kennedy, he was bludgeoned to death by a heavy object, possibly a rock. This is still under investigation and an arrest has been carried out. As to Maitland, he had a dreadful day it seems, he was shot in the kneecap by the drug dealer Rikos Hassan. I will get to that part of the story later. This shooting was confirmed by Jake McCooey. Harvey was also bitten by a snake, but the official cause of his death was by drowning. His crushed legs did not kill him, but he may have passed out in pain prior to breathing in the water. After interviewing the person arrested over the Blaze Kennedy murder, we are of the belief that Harvey may have been involved in the death of Mohammed Khan.'

There was an instant mumble of voices from Marvin's mates in the audience as they realised that at last there may be closure on their mate's demise. Moffitt made no mention of Goliath due to the case still going to court, but many in the audience knew that the bloke Moffitt was talking about was Golly. When the chatter died Moffitt continued.

'In the case of the drug dealer Rikos, he has been on our radar for some time. He died from a spider bite. Possibly a Sydney Funnel Web and his driver an illegal alien formally from Russia, who went by the alias Dmitry, was crushed by a tree limb. It seems nature had a lot of input to the events of that day. Well, that's about it on the criminal case but as to our mate Elvis the Eel, I will hand that over to Nathan from the E.P.A.'

'Thank you, Detective Moffitt, we have had a great deal of discussion about this eel over the past week. At least this time around it did not get the worldwide attention, which it certainly does not deserve. There was no conclusive evidence this so call Elvis had anything more than a carrion involvement in the lake deaths. Although there was the issue that the bite marks on Mr Khan's calf that may have occurred before his death, this was not conclusive enough to warrant the eel's removal from its present situation. The EPA has therefore recommended that we leave it in peace in its natural environment. As to the Aboriginal site, there is a chance that it may get a World Heritage listing. This will provide funds for the Reserve upgrade and possibly a restocking of the biodiversity and a full site feral fencing project. In the meantime, the cave will be secured and fenced off from the public'

Two people in the audience smiled with that report. Jake was delighted that the area would be restored to its former glory and Billy was happy that his old mate was going to hang around a bit longer for some more fishing battles. There were a few more speeches and praise for the locals but as the afternoon went on, refreshments started to win out. The Advisor reporter went off to script a new front page on 'Heroes and Eels.' Bones left for an afternoon shift of solving crimes. Fritz and Mary headed back to the Café and started one of their verbal duels on the nature of people. Everything seemed to be getting back to normal. The afternoon session had evoked into a talkfest on different agendas.

The roasts and bravado in these discussions went on for the rest of the afternoon. Sully was having a go at Jake about all the overtime he missed out on due to the storm damage while he was playing hide and seek in a cave. Jake stirred back over the fact that he had Christmas off again this year and poor old Sully had to work. Meanwhile Charlie Stark took it all in. His story had a wealth of new material now and it was time to write. Bob was giving Steve and Mick the usual lecture on over-indulgence. Billy Chan left to change for the upstairs Karaoke sing along and the Elvis Christmas special, which was due to get underway in about an hour. Most of the pub patrons and their partners were going to the end of year bash and they gathered in the bar until the girls arrived. Moffitt just sat back with a job well done smile on his face and a cold schooner in his hand. An hour later the downstairs crowd were really charged when the filtered sound of Billy Elvis singing 'Suspicious Minds' had them moving upstairs. It was excellent therapy for Jake and Anne who were now looking forward to a family Christmas and a summer holiday.

Moffitt had other plans and headed home. Molly had returned from Perth and the plan for the next day was a ferry trip from Parramatta to Manly, so he wanted a good night's sleep. He had decided to leave his car at the office and catch the bus home. He was not a drink driver. He stepped outside the pub to one of the coldest December nights on record, 'La Nina was up to her old tricks again.' He thought.

Pat Maitland had been thinking about Harvey's death all week. With 'Johnny Walkers' help he was trying to flush his aggression away, but to no avail. Harvey was to be his meal ticket into old age, but that bastard copper and his mates from the pub killed him. Well, that is the way he saw it. As hate boiled and revenge vented from the cauldron that was imbedded in his soul, reprisal thoughts exploded into action.

Moffitt crossed the road and walked towards Palmer Street with a slight beer related swagger to his stride. His every movement was being watched by a concealed figure in a dark recess, adjacent to the Chinese Herb Medicine shop. Pat was now smirking; his victim was fair game. Moffitt heard a noise to his right, but he was too slow to avoid the blow. He raised his right arm, and it took the full force of the pipe. At the same time a gravelly voice was venting anger.

'This one's for you ya bastard!'

Moffitt went to his knees as Pat Maitland raised a section of water pipe above his head for a final blow. Then the words screamed out.

'And this one's for Harvey!' That statement was met with a yelling female voice.

'Drop it Maitland or I'll shoot!'

For a fleeting moment Bones had eye contact with Pat. It was enough for her to realise he was going to continue his onslaught and she fired. In the background Billy could be heard singing 'You're the Devil in Disguise', as the bullet made a muted clang on the water pipe sending Pat's severed thumb sky high with the pipe. Maitland went down in shock, blood spurting in all directions. Bones pushed him face down into the gravel with her foot and as she cuffed him, she checked with Moffitt,

'Are you ok Boss?'

'Yes, thanks mate, nothing broken, probably some bruising that's all. Tell me, how did you know?'

'I was just following up on your request the other day, about keeping an eye on this scumbag. I paid him a visit after signing on. It was getting dark, but as I approached, he came out of the house with the pipe in hand and headed off down the road. I decided to follow him. At first, I thought he was going to cause some damage at Jake's place, but he continued past and towards the pub.

I lost him in the shadows when he crossed over Victoria Road. I have been waiting here and watching for his next move. Sorry I wasn't quick enough to stop the first blow Boss.'

'Don't be, you've done splendid work. Best we wrap that bastards damaged hand, I don't want him to bleed out before he does some jail time.'

Moffitt looked at Maitland with disdain but all he could see was a pathetic old creature leaking blood into the dirt while quivering in hate. It was a picture that summed up a sad wasted life.

CHAPTER 22

Christmas

*'A house becomes a home, not by the
smile of a garden gnome.
But when the sun shines in and visits begin, from
the loved ones you call your own.'*

C hristmas in multi-cultured Parramatta was cele-
brated in a multitude of ways. To some it was
a religious festival, to others it was an excuse for
a holiday, to most it was about feeling good and sharing love. Then there was always the minority who lan-
guished through the whole event with mental or physical
pain. There are people who hate Christmas time for all
the associated stress it brings. It has a mixture of good
and bad blended at times with violence and depression.
Some people spend it by themselves in loneliness and
some prefer it that way. Others will go without presents
and decent food and are happy to spend it with those less
fortunate. The haves and the have nots come to the fore
at Christmas.

Materialism peaks in phase with empathy and drama,

while a good percentage have the love of family around them with its wall of defence. A good example to the above was that while Pat Maitland spent it in a jail cell awaiting conviction and Jim Booth and Charlie Stark wandered in and out the dog kennel of depression, Jake was planning a big family get together based on pure happiness.

Anne and Jake had invited all the family for a Christmas day of fun. The house was in a pre-excitement silence as if contemplating the onset of children's laughter. In the attic dust particles were slowly bouncing amid the rays of mid-morning sunlight, but all was about to change. A tsunami of love and emotion was just exiting the F3 freeway after a slight traffic jam.

Harmony McCooey had built his 'Ravenswood' to last. A door at the end of the stairwell led via six steps to a large pine floored room with narrow gable windows at each end. The room was full of dusty clutter and boxes of memories past.

It was not just Jake and Anne's storage room, the previous solicitor owners had left a plethora of old files and old technology, like typewriters and ribbons. Anne never wished to go into the attic for fear that her cleaning phobia would go into full gear and create weeks of work. Jake had haphazardly re-arranged some of the dusty junk and ran a vacuum cleaner over the see-able surface area when they first purchased the place. The main reason being to make room for his Hornby rail tracks and trains that had grown bit by bit over his life. He often joked that they were the only things his previous wives did not want when it came to settlement issues. He had spent some of his free time in recent months setting up the tracks and tunnels and building little towns and villages. He also had miniature cars, people, and trees. As a boy his Mum and Dad spent nearly a week's wage on his first Hornby rail set, it was the best Christmas present ever. His aim now was to create a replica of the Lakes District in England. It was there, while on holidays in the nineties, he was captivated by the rolling green hills and lakes. 'The Wind in the Willows' was one of his favourite childhood stories and Beatrice Potter was inspired to write it by the areas beauty. The steam train trips in England to quaint villages also added to the inspiration. Whenever the grandchildren came to visit, the first request was to see the trains. If they got the ok nod from grandad, the scramble to be the first one up the stairs began. Most of the time the eldest, Ethan got there first, Hannah came in second and Jacob the youngest ran a close third. The two little ladies Layla and Reeya were generally left crying in the stairwell as victims of the stampede. When the dust settled, and grandad set the trains in motion all was forgiven and the excitement was electric.

A family Christmas get together was long overdue. Anne thought it would help put their lives back into perspective after the recent trauma down at the lake. Both Anne and Jake had received counselling after their short hospital check-up and were told that there may be some post- trauma issues. There were some sleepless nights at first, but their loving relationship was support enough to overcome any deep-seated problems. Moffitt had told them about the incident with Pat Maitland and the possibility of an extended jail term. This was great news for Anne and Jake's security issues and following a search warrant to get some evidence from Pat's rented place, they even got their lawn mower back. But when Moffitt laughed about the lucky shot that sent Maitland's thumb and water-pipe flying high, Jake had a strange feeling of déjà-vu. He smiled along with Moffitt, although for some reason a wave of sadness flushed through him.

Pandemonium broke loose when the tribe of grandkids arrived. Jake was in the attic setting up some extra landscapes around one of the train stations when he heard the footsteps on the stairs. The door flew open and to his surprise Reeya and Layla, who for once had beaten the crowd, came rushing in with the happy glow and the vocal shout of 'Grandad!' This always made his heart skip a beat with pride. Reeya had in her hand a recent award for excellence in Jazz Ballet. Beaming with the thrill of achievement she had passed it to Jake. At the same moment there was a rush of air as Jacob, Hannah and Ethan charged in. The certificate became air borne and drifted across the room seemingly with a will of its own. It came to rest on the far wall and slipped behind an old shipping crate. Jake saw Reeya's smile fade into pre-tear turmoil.

The old box was full of the discarded and 'may-be-useful-one-day' trinkets. It had the look of a heavy permanent fixture that had been topped up over the last hundred years with rusty old doorknobs, hinges nails and unwanted tools. He tried to move the box with Ethan's help, but it would not budge. They had two choices. Empty it of its collective memories or lever it aside. An old canoe paddle did the trick as they managed to move the box about a foot before the certificate floated out. While Jake was praising the Ballet effort, Ethan and Hannah were focused on the box of junk.

'What's behind that door Grandad?' Hannah asked, pointing to rear of the box.

All eyes in the attic, except those of young Jacob, turned

with the lure of discovery. Young Jacob was still in a world of moving trains. Jake levered the box another foot for a better look and sure enough there was a door.

'I have no idea!' He responded as the excitement rose.

The small door built into the wall cavity had rusted hinges and a bolted clip. Jake took a crowbar and managed to get it open. As all the wide eyes looked on, Jake reached in and removed a small timber box smothered in dust. He cleaned the box with an old rag. It revealed a well-made mahogany antique with an Irish family crest embossed on the lid. Jake sat back with the box on his lap knowing they had discovered something incredibly special. The children gathered around urging him to open it. This coincided with a call from Anne.

'Jake, Christmas dinner is being served, come and cut the roast!'

There was a collective sigh of disappointment when Jake said,

'Well, the whole family should witness its opening and we will do that straight after lunch.'

Lunch was one of Anne's usual massive feasts. It could have fed fifty and was dished out to only twenty. Jake placed the box in the middle of the table, and it stole all the Christmas wonder, even the presents were forgotten. While everyone ate, the thoughts were flying. All the girls thought it would contain love letters and jewellery. The boys were less circumspect, they said it was probably just a special tool like a micrometre or something similar. The grandkids did not care, they just wanted it opened.

Finally, the moment came. Jake slowly opened the box with the help of a knife to cut the candle wax seal. As the audience looked on there was a sudden sense of bewilderment, two items came into view, one was a leather-bound journal, and the other was a darkened glass jar with a sealed lid and containing a liquid. Jake held the jar to the light and said with a bemused expression on his face.

'It's a thumb!'

The kids quickly lost interest; the Christmas presents were now the focus of their attention. As Anne looked over his shoulder Jake was carefully turning the pages of the journal. It was very fragile, and time had done its damage. Although written in Old English, with 'f' as an 's' and other quirks of the times, it was still readable. One entry got his instant attention, it was the story of how Harmony lost his thumb. The irony of Moffitt's mention of the thumb was not missed. This grew into total amazement when he read on to find that a fellow named Pug Maitland was his ancestor's nemesis on the voyage. The whole family would eventually hear of Harmony's full story and the connection of foes across time would always be a source of wonder, but for now the day was for the living.

There were Christmas wrappings from one side of the room to the other when Jake finally put the journal and the thumb bottle away, to be studied on another occasion. But the entry on the last page was to remain in his thoughts, it read.

'Fear can be an enemy or a friend, use it as a friend when you fear your enemy.'

CHAPTER 23

Summer

The year had been filled to overflowing with drama, mystery, and excitement. Jake and Anne both needed a break just to help put things into perspective. Down the track they would be able to read Charlie Stark's novel about their world, which may help. But for now, they just wanted to reflect. It was hard to think about Marvin's demise, Elvis the eel and Moffitt without thinking how close they had come to being just memories.

The latest news from Moffitt was disturbing. Pat Maitland's Sorrell Street house had become a crime scene. Bones had made some enquiries into the owners of the property following the search warrant. Pham Quang and his wife Ly had not been seen for several months. The minister at the local Cabramatta church had also contacted police. He was concerned that they had not returned from Vietnam and the matter was on a police file. Bones found out from Customs that the Phams never left the country. Forensics were called in to inspect the Sorrell Street house. Quang and Ly were found buried in the backyard garden under two withering trees. They were bound together, with obvious knife wounds. It was a sad end for a happy loving couple. The scene was awash with evidence that Patrick Maitland had murdered them, and that Harvey may have assisted. Heartless Pat it seemed would now get free board and food for the rest of his pitiful life.

Some of the other problems in Jake's life had been resolved and settled as well. Layla's tumour was removed and found to be benign. Lisa had decided to move to Nelson Bay for a fresh start after she and Layla's father broke up. Stan and his wife Lidia continued to struggle bringing up four children on basic wages. Their outlays always outstripped funds like in most modern families. Jake had seen this all before when he was younger. He persisted with the argument of enjoying the moment and forgoing the credit. Deaf ears meant more struggle in the future, but for now all was well. Anne's mum had settled in well at the nursing home and seemed to be happy. Even Jake's step boys Dirk and Ralf had been in contact.

As for Jake and Anne, life was rolling along like a meandering stream. They had booked a European vacation for the following year and retirement for them both was just around the corner. Life at the Rose and Thorn went on as normal and best of all Steve and Cheryl had booked out the whole pub for their wedding next April. One of the most amazing turn of events and character, concerned Fritz. He had started going out with Bill's Chinese cousin Lilly. It seems the multi-culture soup does have potential.

'Yes,' thought Jake. 'LIFE, the acronym for human behaviour, Love Intensely and Forgive Easily, just about summed it up. But sadly, it would be exceedingly difficult to forgive the Maitland types. Greed and violence would probably always lie close by in the shadows of those dark and fearful places'

They awoke to their first morning at Anne's sister's seaside caravan to a cacophony of noise. Jake had another of his strange dreams and relayed it to Anne before it was lost. Parts of it involved his escape from a deep dark cavern and to exit onto a pristine beach. It was a still sunny day; the ocean was bright blue, and the sand was as white as chalk. There was a line of children holding hands and the line extended for the length of the beach. They were girls and boys no older than four and representing all the races on Earth. Without exception they were all smiling and laughing with one foot in the water and one foot on the sand. All he could sense was empathy and love, the one thought that stood out to Jake was the lack of prejudice.

'All part of the healing process dear,' proclaimed Anne, sensing his puzzlement.

'Let's get some breakfast.'

Shoal Bay was always busy at this time of year. There were children crying, kookaburras laughing and the clanging of a garbage truck picking up the happy campers trash. The trash smell dissipated quickly and was replaced with the mouth-watering odour of bacon cooking. While Anne did the bulk of the work in breakfast preparation, Jake wandered off down to the water's edge.

'A perfect day,' he thought.

The large trees and white sand encompassed a sparkling blue bay. There was no wind, and the water was still, except for the low waves that lapped at Jake's feet. This place was truly a wonderland. Two magnificent mountain peaks guarding the harbour's entrance added to the magic. The local Aboriginals of the Worimi Tribe had inhabited the Port Stephens area when the tall ships came. They were noted to be fairer in skin colour and of taller and stouter build than other Aborigines. They had named these mountains Tomaree and Yaccaba. There was a connection here and he could feel it in the soft sand and the cool water on this very spot on the beach. He had read Harmony's journal and for all he knew this could be the exact location that his ancestor had stepped ashore for the first time. It gave him an overwhelming sense of completion in the cycles of settlement.

Jake headed back to the van. They were both now active and well awake and got stuck into the morning feast. After breakfast and a walk up Tomaree Mountain they headed off to the Salamander Bay shopping centre. Anne's idea was to do a quick shop before the heat of day and head back for a swim. This plan hit the wall when they joined the throng of Christmas holiday traffic all with the same idea, the best part of their day was lost. Two hours later they arrived back at the van just in time for lunch and a choir of cicadas. It was hot and still; the van temperature was thirty-four degrees.

'It's time for that swim Anne!'

'Let's go Jake, it's like an oven in here.' The crystal-clear water of the bay seemed to be shouting at them to cool off. They swam to a sand bar and watched the whiting scatter on the clean sandy bottom.

'It doesn't get any better than this!' Anne said, with a blissful expression.

'Yes, it does babe. Remember that great camping holiday we had in Victoria a couple of years back? I remember you saying Apollo Bay and Buchan Caves were the prettiest spots in Australia.'

'That was then Jake, and this is now. By the way Australia has a glut of great spots and as far as I'm concerned, I have had my fill of caves.'

'I think I will agree with you on that one, today this is the best spot in Oz, if only that thunderhead stays where it is.'

Looking westward there was a large mass of billowing clouds. When they got back to shore the eerie still of a balmy day was suddenly broken by the crack of distant thunder. They towelled off and started heading back to the van, passing a traffic-jam of boats at the ramp. Everyone now seemed to be aware of the pending tempest. There was a surreal feeling of expectation in the air, as campers and day trippers seemed to quicken their activity. The summer storm continued to brew.

'This is really weird.' Jake mused. 'All these wet swimmers are heading back from a sun-drenched beach to avoid getting wet.'

They arrived back at the van and while Jake cracked a beer and poured Anne a wine, she put together a cheese platter as a treat for the pending theatre. The eerie still and the cicada din came to an end with a sudden breeze. Tarps flapped and deck chairs flew. Branches and raindrops played a rat-a-tat-tat on the van roof and Jake turned up the volume on the radio to hear the cricket. For some unknown reason, the fear of the storm faded with the excitement of being secure and relaxed.

A burning bright rip in the sky above and an instant cannon roar of thunder had heads peering out of tents and vans to witness the carnage. A smouldering tree branch imbedded in a vacant late model sedan turned up the volume of excitement to a new high. The distraught owner of the damaged vehicle was seen shaking his fist at the sky and cursing, as he ran around wet with rain telling all his neighbours about his current nightmare. Jake was watching their startled faces as they made bland suggestions to unsuccessfully ease the victim's anxiety. Jake offered a tarp to cover up the gaping hole in the roof of the car and tried to settle the man with 'a glass half full' suggestion,

'You know mate it would have been worse if you had been in the car.'

This seemed to tame the man's stress a little.

The storm continued, the rain fell harder, and the hail gave it a climax. The cricket was no longer audible and the last word that Jake heard was, 'Ponting was out for a duck.' Ducks were the only thing missing, as a river was now flowing around the van and down the road. The hail had changed the landscape to that of a European winter white out. Anne sat reading, wine glass half empty and a soft smile on her face. She was feeling safe in her cocoon of steel and far removed from natures outside protest. Another strike! Another startled look as a sound wave rocked the van and Anne topped up her wine glass. The rain calmed to a steady shower. Howzat! Another wicket fell as the radio came back into hearing range. Jake got himself another beer.

'I love Christmas holidays,' said Jake, as he peered out the door beyond the moat of cool water around the perceived safety of their caravan castle. To the east thunderclaps and lightning moved on, like a sweeping broom impervious to man.

'Would you like some leg ham and salad for dinner, Jake?'

'Sounds great, guess what? the temperature in here is

down to twenty-three degrees. I might go fishing tomorrow and catch a 'big-un'!'

'Keep it pan size dear, I've had my fill of 'big-un's' and 'gentle giants'!'

'Jake? Could you turn the cricket off now and put on that Elvis Christmas disc Billy gave us?'

'I may as well babe, we are well and truly out of this test. What we need is another Warnie. Still, it will not be long before we add a Soccer World Cup to our trophy room. Our multinational talent pool and tolerance is getting deeper by the year.'

'I think you're right Jake, maybe even at the shallow end!'

Life back at the Lake Reserve in Parramatta was slowly returning to normal. Nature, the master of destruction and repair was making restitution. It may take a couple of years for the reserve to return to its former glory, but eventually new growth will sprout, and new tracks will be trodden. Then life and order will find a balance, and people of all races and gather.

Future visitors to the lake will read a sign near the old swimming beach, that says:

'Swim at your own risk – the eels may bite!'

On which a local graffiti artist will paint, 'Elvis Lives.'

There may also be the occasional fisherman trying his luck in this lake, at the head of a river, that flows to Parramatta, a place:

Where the Eels lie down.

CHAPTER 24

Where travellers met

L ike dew on winter grass, the perspiration glistened on Harmony's face:
  'Put your backs into it,' the captain yelled! 'I want you felons back in the ship's belly by night fall'.

With a shrewd face that bespoke a hardened heart and a razor-sharp sabre that expressed authority, Captain Melville stood tall at the small boat's bow.

'McCooey, you and Jenkins make ready to secure the boat when we land. And don't be thinking you can scarper off like a couple of fleas, Elliot's over there and he is a crack shot. The natives around here could be cannibals so keep your eyes open.'

Harmony knew full well the danger of his present situation. The crew was nervous and not averse to taking their fear out on one of us. As to the natives eating habits, at this stage he would take the captain's word for it.

'Be alert lads!' The captain hushed.

Harmony synchronised his rowing with the other convicts as his eyes scanned the shoreline

'A perfect day,' he thought. The sun reflected off white sand and a blue bay that encompassed a forest of huge strange looking trees. This place was truly a wonderland. Two magnificent mountain peaks guarding the harbours entrance caused Harmony to reflect to his beloved Ireland and the Ardglass harbour near his home.

'Captain?' Harmony begged.

'Can I have permission to speak sir?'

'Go ahead McCooey but keep it brief.'

Captain Melville knew of Harmony from the Maitland incident and believed his story. Since then, the convicts on board were given a little more deck time and Harmony's good character reference had filtered up the ranks. The ship's officers and even Mr Friend had grown accustomed to McCooey's curiosity of things and occasionally tolerated his questions.

'What place is this Sir?'

'It's listed on the charts as Port Stephens, named by Cook in 1770, but just keep your mind on the job at hand and I'll worry about where we are!' he quipped. 'We're here for water and repairs only, the southerly storm last night blew us off course, so we are some distance north of Sydney Cove. I know of this port; it has already been settled further inland. They bring the cedar down for direct shipment to England.'

They raised their oars and approached the beach. With a good eye for things out of place, Harmony noticed movement at the foot of one of the giant trees. It was as if the tree suddenly grew arms. In a second of surprising reflex Harmony let fly with the oar, knocking the captain overboard into the shallow water. At the same moment, a spear with the captain's name on it, skewed Jenkin's leg to the gunnels of the boat. Jenkins screamed in pain, as some of the crew watched on in fear.

'What the hell McCooey!' Melville shouted, as he stood shaking the water off in a rattle of demure defiance.

'There is sir, by the tree' Harmony pointed.

Quickly the Captain composed himself and yelled,

'Load and fire Elliot, shoot that black devil.'

'Yes sir' was the response, as the instinct of a trained soldier kicked in.

Within seconds and in one movement the flint ignited, and the gun fired. The shot missed its target and the black man fled in puzzled fear, as the white's sound of terror echoed across the pristine bay.

Captain Melville was impressed with the way McCooey saved him from the spear. He even offered a letter to the Governor which canvassed a reduced sentence. There was light on the horizon for Harmony. As he stood there on the white sandy beach in the shadow of those two magnificent peaks, awaiting the order to board, he reflected on life. The only connection to the past now was the vast ocean of water that he had crossed. What lay ahead in the future was unknown, but he had a sense that all would be well. For some unknown reason he could feel it in the soft sand and the cool water of this beach, with its connection to this great southern land.

ABOUT THE AUTHOR

Gary John Carter

I was born in July 1952 in Western Sydney, a lucky time to be alive. I worked in the Electrical supply industry. I have lived a basic suburban life and avoided the stepping-stones of strife. I planted a few trees as my houses turned to homes. I had a son and a daughter, and I am also blessed with grandchildren. I love to tell stories and now I have authored some books.

Now my days are now running faster I am grateful for the cause and effect granted by the 'Big Bangs' master.

BOOKS BY THIS AUTHOR

About That Shout

The history of Pubs, Inns and Hostelries in Parramatta. The book contains an account of past and present hotels and inns of Parramatta, and some of the stories within, dating from 1800 to the present.

ISBN: 978-0-9953680-0-2

The Cull

From the pristine waters off Tasmania, to the streets of multicultural Parramatta, in a world now battered by climate change and the Covid-19 pandemic, we are challenged to face the inevitable. Marlin Jackson a boy prodigy receives a message from a fifth dimensional life form called the MUZE. Their time is non-linear, as infinite as the size of our universe, and at a right angle to our perception abilities. With their help Jackson may find an answer, but we are a resource driven species destined for extinction and we are eight billion too many. Their invitation has been sent, acceptance is pending, and it is not negotiable.

Arnold Bask is a pioneer, in a space-time device called

the Object, built by Jackson's company. Arnold 's mind becomes the conduit for the MUZE on their journey of assessment around Sydney. Arnold walks into a Parramatta pub his first glance was on Rachelle Castles, and his heart skips a beat. The MUZE within his mind discover an experience long gone from their collective memories. Human love is a powerful force, but was it enough to stop the CULL

ISBN: 978-0-9953680-3-3